THE VIEW FROM THE LANE

THE VIEW FROM THE LANE
& OTHER STORIES

DEBORAH-ANNE TUNNEY

Copyright © 2014 Deborah-Anne Tunney

Enfield & Wizenty
(an imprint of Great Plains Publications)
233 Garfield Street
Winnipeg, MB R3G 2M1
www.greatplains.mb.ca

All rights reserved. No part of this publication may be reproduced or transmitted in any form or in any means, or stored in a database and retrieval system, without the prior written permission of Great Plains Publications, or, in the case of photocopying or other reprographic copying, a license from Access Copyright (Canadian Copyright Licensing Agency), 1 Yonge Street, Suite 1900, Toronto, Ontario, Canada, M5E 1E5.

Great Plains Publications gratefully acknowledges the financial support provided for its publishing program by the Government of Canada through the Canada Book Fund; the Canada Council for the Arts; the Province of Manitoba through the Book Publishing Tax Credit and the Book Publisher Marketing Assistance Program; and the Manitoba Arts Council.

Design & Typography by Relish New Brand Experience

Printed in Canada by Friesens

Library and Archives Canada Cataloguing in Publication

Tunney, Deborah-Anne, author
    The view from the lane / Deborah-Anne Tunney.

Short stories.
Issued in print and electronic formats.
ISBN 978-1-927855-02-7 (pbk.).--ISBN 978-1-927855-03-4 (epub).--ISBN 978-1-927855-04-1 (mobi)

    I. Title.

PS8639.U56V54 2014   C813'.6   C2014-903357-5
                                               C2014-903358-3

For my mother
Ethel May Tunney

What are we but snow's endless fall…
    —Jiri Orten
    "What Are We?"

If the door were open, I'd listen to creek water
And think I heard voices from long ago
    distinct, and calling me home

The past becomes such a mirror —we're in it, and then we're not
    —Charles Wright
    "On the Night of the First Snow, Thinking about Tennessee"

TABLE OF CONTENTS

Overture | 11
Nelson Street | 13
Aura | 36
Her Mother's Daughter | 40
First Snow | 49
The Wedding | 54
Studebaker | 73
Us Dogs | 89
My Brother's Condition | 99
The View from the Lane | 111
Suicide Notes | 120
The Murder on Prince Albert Street | 144
On the Bus | 154
Worst Snowstorm of the Year | 162
A Nasty Bit of Business | 176
Toadhead | 193
Visitations | 202
Evandie | 211
Weekend | 222

OVERTURE

Look there, beneath us, snow falls on the street of red brick houses. We can see the peaks of their roofs and hear cars grumbling under the snow, their wipers creating intersecting arcs while the headlights cut cone-shaped light into the space before them. A young girl looks out the upstairs window of one of the duplexes. In the room where she stands, her mother sits in front of a mirror, fingering the pearls of her necklace, each pearl a memory. She hums a song from the early 1920s, from her own childhood, when she lived with her brothers and sisters in a large house in an old Ottawa neighbourhood, more than thirty-five years before. The girl's father lies in the bed beside the vanity where the mother sits, adrift in his pained sleep.

Stray dogs roam the back alley; it is a neighbourhood for stray dogs. A man walks along the street, hands shoved in his pockets, head bent, slanted against the storm. The wind gusts and snow whitens the distance. The girl at the window follows his progress as he becomes a stroke of black against white. In the living room downstairs a sister and two brothers watch the grainy image on a black and white television; we see them illuminated by its flickering grey light. The girl at the upstairs window is four years old and it is 1956.

Amy stands by the window and looks at the snow falling on the parking lot of her mother's nursing home; a white absence spreads across the field. Such scenes always evoke the storms from the winter of her father's death. Throughout the years, as a teenager walking to school, as a young woman in her twenties watching from a bus on her way to work, or as a mother and wife living in a small town outside Ottawa, the soft fall of snow would always still her thoughts, bring her back to where she could see the streets of her childhood and sense in the scene an isolating quiet. Now fifty years later, it is snowing again. Amy watches it drift into silence when a sudden weariness overtakes her.

The surrounding fields brim with drifts of snow; at the line of houses beyond, smoke from the chimneys rises grey against a paler grey sky, as the sound of her mother's laboured breathing fills the room. In the window's reflection, she can see her sister standing by the bed. All the moments of their mother's life gather here, the childhood in the first decade of the twentieth century, the years of her children, and the times she shared with people who are gone and those who will remain. The room is warm, crowded with memories and shadows. Amy places her hand on the window's metal frame, is grateful for the cold under her palm and for the frost that crawls along the pane in a ghostly quartz pattern, mathematical and important in its miniature beauty.

NELSON STREET

More than eighty years ago, the Howard family lived on Nelson Street in the center of Ottawa, close to the university, in an area known as Sandy Hill. There were ten children in the family, not an uncommonly large number for the time. The firstborn, a girl, died of scarlet fever when she was six years old, and her mother, although she seldom spoke of the death, never forgot the day her first child died. At times throughout the years as she raised her children, heard their rambunctious talk and arguments she'd see her young daughter, perpetually six, sitting on the front porch looking out to the road, or standing at the top of the staircase as she herself mounted the steps after another tiring day. It was no surprise, then, that near the end of her life, when she was in her early seventies, delusional and ill, she saw this child dressed in the blue-and-white sundress she had been buried in, watching her dying mother from the end of the bed.

The last year that all nine Howard children, five boys and four girls, aged four to twenty-two, had lived in the same house was 1920. The road in front of their house was made from hardened mud and gravel, and during the summer, when the tall windows were open, the sound of horses pulling carts and wagons could be heard through the high-ceilinged rooms. The pale light of early evening settled into these rooms and the upstairs hallways, stretching through the space in dusty bands. It was this large house with its many windows, either open to the air or closed and reflecting the light, that years later the children remembered best, after they'd moved away—those windows and the early-morning smell of the honeysuckle bushes that lined the side yard.

On the first floor was a kitchen, where the mother spent many hours making meals or sitting by the fireplace mending worn socks and threadbare pants. In the hottest weeks of July and August, the stove would be moved to the summer kitchen at the back of the house. The dining room table was big enough to seat twenty, which it often did on Sundays when the children brought friends home. Across the hall was the living room, where the father read his paper in the evenings, and a den where he would retire every working day after lunch for his noon nap. Because they were coaxed by their mother to be quiet during these nap periods, the children, who had a desire to please their mother—a kind woman who made each child feel special—came to regard their father as a nuisance.

The last year the whole family lived together, the girls, aged six to fifteen, sitting side by side at the dinner table, were distinguished by their size and the colour of their hair, hair that had been combed smooth down their backs—Margaret's dark auburn, Rita's blonde, Dorothy's red and June's almost black, the same colour as her father's.

Each of the children at one time or another heard the story of how their mother and father met. Usually their mother as she sat sewing or mending would recount the day of their meeting without looking up, as if it were a song or poem long remembered and greatly valued. The mother's family had been wealthy and lived in Westmount, in Montreal. They owned a number of hotels in the city and the father had been appointed manager of one of them. At Christmas of the year the mother turned twenty, he was invited to a dinner party at the home of his employer. The father said he had only to see her once, to see her cross the room, the sway of her dress, the smile as she turned, extending her hand when they were introduced, for his life to be changed forever. At this point in the story, the mother would look up, perhaps thinking how much that moment was responsible for the scene before her, for the children in the room listening to her, for those children she could hear upstairs, and for her husband, who was most often beside her reading his newspaper.

Over the years the mother became stately, so that when people referred to her they called her handsome, or they would remark how, when she was young, she must have been a great beauty. In the evenings after the younger children had slipped off to bed she would join her husband by the fire in the living room, and for hours as the light dimmed no sound intruded, except the occasional rustle of newspaper, and the click of her knitting needles. Later in their lives, the children would remember their parents best like this, not speaking, yet connected, each pursuing a private interest.

In the years before June began school, a widow who lived on the same block made a point of greeting the father in the afternoons when he would walk by her on his way home from work. She had black hair and wore red lipstick. "Daniel," she would say with a nod of her head and a smile. In the summer, if she were in the garden when he passed, as she often seemed to be, she would pick a rose and give it to him. Once, after accepting the flower and saying something about the beauty of roses and the beauty of women, he looked up and saw June, six at the time, face clouded with anger. When he asked what she had done that day, she refused to speak to him. June told her mother about this woman, how she waited in her front yard in order to speak with her father, and how she would smile with her "big fat lips." But the mother only laughed and said, "Well, aren't you the little spy?"

※

In order to find work during the Depression, the boys of the family, except for the youngest, moved to Detroit and never lived in Canada again. She seldom spoke of the loss, but at Christmas the mother would look around the table as fewer and fewer of her children congregated there, and she would seem depleted. Instead of having more of herself to give her daughters, she appeared to have less. In the years just after the departure of her oldest son, a man of exceptional good looks who would have a successful career as a litigator in Michigan, her health began to decline when she was diagnosed with heart disease. By the time she died, the four sisters' memories were mostly of their mother sad and withdrawn; they all said, when remembering her, that life had taken its toll.

When the girls were in their teens they quit school one by one to work in the beauty salon at the Chateau Laurier, a large hotel beside the Parliament buildings, located off Confederation Square, or Confusion Square, as it was informally known. An imposing stone building with turrets and gothic spires, it had an impressive salon that took up most of the mezzanine level. They were pretty girls, clever with their hands, so they quickly graduated from being receptionists or mixing hair colour to doing facials and manicures. At the time, cutting hair was reserved for male hairdressers.

By the time she was in her early twenties, the eldest daughter, Margaret, was head manicurist and kept the agenda of the salon. A slim, intelligent woman with long graceful hands, quick to laugh, she had an easy way about her that made her one of the favourites of the clientele and the salon's owner, who knew he had found a treasure. Near the end of a working day in May 1926, a man appeared before her at the receptionist's desk, wanting a haircut, and she brought him to the back room to wash his hair, preparing him, as was her job, for one of the male hairdressers. She softly hummed "Heart of my Heart," a song popular at the time. He was a wealthy New Yorker, the heir of a large business machine company, in Canada on a business trip. On this day, as he reclined in the salon chair, looking up at Margaret's hands, at the sure, strong way they moved and feeling the warmth of the water and her fingertips on his scalp, he wanted to stop them, or so he told her later, to turn them over and kiss their soft inner palms, palms that smelled of lemons. When he asked her her name and she told him, he said his name was Bradley, and she nodded and quickly forgot.

The next morning when Margaret arrived at the front desk and sat checking the agenda and making notes for the hairdressers, he suddenly appeared before her. She told her sisters that when she looked up, there was something so endearing about him that although she had many boyfriends and was not initially attracted to him, in an instant she became aware of him in a new way, a way that made her look closely at his boyish smile and be charmed by his shy manner. Within three months they were married, and over the six years they lived together, before he died unexpectedly from a brain aneurism, she came to learn that despite his competence in most things he was incapable of standing up to his mother. And so with these battles left to Margaret, she fought with her mother-in-law over most major decisions in their domestic lives, the houses and furniture they would buy, where they would live and vacation. Weary from the conflict and from her husband's increasing withdrawal, she grew to wonder if it was Bradley she loved or their life together and the privilege his money allowed them.

During their marriage they divided their time between the United States and Canada, where they bought a summer home across the river from Ottawa in Aylmer, so that Margaret's family could visit on weekends. She wore tailored trousers and silk blouses bought from designers in New York City, smoked cigarettes through a long holder and decorated her homes with expensive furniture, sheers between stiff brocade drapes, floors covered with oriental carpets. In her apartment in New York City, a down-filled chesterfield covered in navy blue silk dominated the living room and eighteenth century paintings lined the satin covered walls. For the rest of her life, even when she was growing old and delusional, she could close her eyes and see this room and feel the pride she felt when she created it, even though living there meant she no longer participated in the only family life she'd ever known with her parents and siblings in that sprawling house on Nelson Street.

A year after her marriage, Margaret woke one morning in Ottawa with excruciating pain in her abdomen and was rushed to the hospital. After an operation for an ectopic pregnancy, she was told she would not be able to have children, and despite the sympathy from her sisters, sympathy which she listened to and accepted quietly, she was secretly glad to know her life would not be altered to accommodate a child. But without an heir to cement her claim to her husband's name and fortune, after Bradley's sudden death Margaret was given just a yearly annuity and the Aylmer home. She settled there and never again saw her New York apartment or her mother-in-law, who secretly believed that somehow Margaret had caused Bradley's aneurism.

Two years later in the office of the lawyer who looked after her trust, Margaret met her second husband, a jovial, wealthy man named Philip. After their marriage they moved to Montreal where Philip's family ran a steel manufacturing business. There Margaret developed the habit of drinking every evening and spending her days recuperating from parties they'd thrown the night before. But this version of her life also ended when Philip died from pancreatic cancer, so that by the early 1960s, she had moved back to Ottawa to be close to her sisters. At first she lived in the house in Aylmer, which she had kept and visited over the years, but within a few months, because she found the house too large and remote, she moved to the city. By this point her mother was dead, her father lived in Florida with his second wife and the house on Nelson Street had long since been converted to a boarding house for students. When the Howard family had lived there, the rooms had been decorated in floral wallpaper with high crown and floor mouldings, those same walls that now were sullied to the colour of soiled linen and stripped of adornment except posters and bulletin boards. Over the years whenever the sisters drove by their old house, they found it difficult to see any vestige from their young lives in the collection of bicycles cluttering the side lane or the students they saw sitting on the veranda where they themselves had sat with their parents so many years before.

The year of Margaret's first marriage, Dorothy, at eighteen, was working in the salon, where she was a manicurist and mixed the dyes used to colour hair. A careful woman, she became the dependable heart of the salon: the first person to arrive in the morning, turning on the lights and starting the coffee urn, and often the last person to leave in the evening. Engaged from the age of seventeen to a boy who lived on the same block, she was a silent help to her mother around the house, making sure her younger sisters and brothers were fed and bathed or ready for school. She longed for the routine of a domestic life with her own children and home, so when she was twenty-one and no closer to marriage, she asked her boyfriend one spring night if he still intended to marry her. She always wondered if she had not asked if he would have admitted he had fallen in love with her best friend, a petite blonde girl who was popular and always seemed to be laughing. They were on the veranda of her house on Nelson Street, and she said simply, "I see," turning from him. To her back he said he would always have fond memories and think well of her and the years they had been together. After he left, as the night came down around her, Dorothy sat on the swing, alone in the dark, and hoped that if she did not move maybe the conversation would never have happened. If she could clear her mind of his words, then perhaps she could convince herself that they had never been spoken.

In the months to follow, she continued her schedule of waking at six a.m., looking after her youngest sister, walking to the hotel, speaking to her fellow workers and completing the tasks that she had learned and performed since she had started working there. No one could have guessed, watching her quiet competence, how she was reliving that night. She had not cried; she was too numb and unsure; even weeks later she found it difficult to believe that evening had happened. The sadness settled in her with such weight that she lost all expectation of ever being content again.

A year later another boy who lived in the neighbourhood, a boy she had always considered too young and awkward, called and asked her to the movies. They went to a theatre on Rideau Street, not far from her home, and whenever she recalled the evening to one of her sisters or later, to her daughter, she always mentioned the yellow sundress she wore that her mother had made, how it showed off her arms and neck, two of her best features. By autumn Dorothy and Joseph, this new suitor, were engaged and by the winter of 1932, married. As was common for married women at the time, and much to the disappointment of everyone at the salon, she quit her job. She and her husband moved into a small, two-bedroom apartment, close to her parents' house and began a routine that included Monday cleaning, Tuesday shopping and Sunday dinner at Nelson Street. During the summer months, Sundays were spent at her sister's house in Aylmer, sitting out on the lawn looking across the river as the soft glow of city lights and the stars grew distinct against a darkening sky.

It took Dorothy many long and anxious years to become pregnant with her only child, a daughter, whom she named Sophia after her maternal grandmother. Dorothy often took Sophia in the stroller to visit her own mother during the afternoons and was sometimes still there when June returned from work. Always interested in the news from the salon, Dorothy would ask her sister what had happened that day, shaking her head or laughing at what June told her and when walking home she would think how she missed the place, the sense of competence and relevance she received from working there. Because Joseph's job, as the manager of an oil distribution office, demanded that they move, Dorothy and her husband eventually left Ottawa, and even though each move brought with it larger, more expensive houses, she always remembered those early years of her marriage as the happiest of her life.

Much later, when she was in the hospital near the end of her life, it was not the salon of the Chateau Laurier that came back to her but the bright-windowed rooms of the house on Nelson Street, the Sunday evenings when the family used to gather around the table for dinner, the rush in the morning as each of her brothers and sisters got ready for the day, or the quiet way her mother and father sat in the evening listening to the radio in the living room. These moments repeated in her mind with a potent familiarity, like a song, impossible to forget.

※

When Dorothy married Joseph and quit the salon, she left her two younger sisters, Rita and June, working there. June was only fifteen, but in those days it was not uncommon to start working that young. Rita was the receptionist, who looked after the ordering of supplies for the hairdressers, which meant that she knew all the salesmen who came to the salon selling beauty products. Edgar, one of these salesmen, caught her interest; he was nervous in a way that made him appear ambitious and serious, and he never made overtures to Rita, something that annoyed but at the same time attracted her. She was blonde and voluptuous, and as she worked she gave off an air of boundless energy and enthusiasm so that you could often hear her laughter and chatter from the other rooms of the salon. Rita knew her sisters had husbands with futures, and it seemed to her that this man, attractive though he was, lacked refinement; she could not imagine him sitting at the family dining room table as the boyfriends or husbands of her sisters did, contributing to the conversation and impressing her father. It took almost a year until she brought him home, but by that time she was in love and did not care what her father or sisters might think. She need not have worried because he not only impressed her father but also went on to impress the owner of the company where he worked, becoming top salesman and eventually vice president.

By the time their first child was born, they were living off Island Park Drive in the west end of Ottawa, where she had two more children and where they lived for twenty more years until Edgar admitted one night in late 1958 that he was in love with his secretary and was leaving. After a few months during which time she continued to withdraw from her family, she was placed in a private psychiatric hospital in the Laurentians, where she followed a schedule of meals, appointments with her doctor and solitary walks along trails that meandered through the countryside. When her sisters would visit, they brought her to the sunroom, talked about their children or brothers, how they had decorated their living rooms or how winter was coming early that year. Rita looked past them to the window, but they would continue, convinced that what she really needed was to care about these things again. After nine months, when she came back to Ottawa, she did not return to the house she had shared with her husband but moved instead into one of the first high-rise apartment buildings of the city, on Riverside Drive.

When she first moved to the apartment it was with her youngest son, a senior in high school. Her two other children had married and left home and the new quietness at the core of her life left her with time to reflect on how it was she ended up there, unmarried, living a life where she found her greatest comfort from women—her sisters whom she called often and friends she met who were divorced or widowed. Within a few years, her daughter Claire had a baby and Rita often spent her afternoons with them while Claire's husband was at work. But as soon as he returned home, Rita would leave, saying when he coaxed her to stay, "No, no, you young ones need your time alone." It came to feel to Rita as if her life was half-lived, full of talk and television and the sense, if she was being honest, of emptiness. If she had tried to explain her life since Nelson Street she would have said the plans she had made, the happiness she had coveted, those goals were unrealistic and ultimately unattainable. Over the years when she would sit on the balcony watching the stream of cars and river below, she'd think how her life had changed, its patterns and routines unrecognizable to her younger self, the girl who had been part of that large family in that large house on Nelson Street, a few miles from where she now sat.

⚭

June met her first husband, William, at school when she was fourteen and he was sixteen, a few months before she began working in the salon. Shy, she spent her breaks and lunch hour with her sister Dorothy, who taught her the routine of the salon, how to mix dyes, greet clients and take appointments. June married William in her early twenties and shortly after moved to Montreal, where his skills as a carpenter were used in the war effort. When they first lived there, they were happy, but as the years went by and June had her second child, William began to stay out later and later with his coworkers, and June began to feel more and more alone and isolated. William became ill with tuberculosis, which made it necessary for the family to move back to Ottawa and stay with his parents, the only relatives who had the room to take them in. He died of consumption before the war ended, and June, who had also been infected, was forced to stay in a sanatorium for more than a year. Her children, aged four and six, went to live with different relatives—Natalie with Dorothy and her son Lawrence with her brother, Norman, and his wife. June could only see her children on Sundays and only through the glass panes dividing the visiting room, looking very much, she thought, like a prisoner's visiting room, with chairs and phones on either side of the windows. The children were always dressed in their best clothes, Natalie's blonde hair in ringlets, Lawrence wearing a bowtie; they would sit before the window, taking turns speaking to their mother over the phone. When June later recalled her illness, she always said the hardest part was not being able to touch her children.

At the end of her ward was a sunroom with worn sofas, bookcases stacked with newspapers, used books and, in the corner, under the window, an old piano. One day when she went there to read she found a young man playing the song "Sentimental Journey," and the melody stayed with her long after he had stopped playing and left the room. The next day when he was there again, she asked him to play the song. He looked up and said, "You have remarkable eyes." She used to say if they had not met in a sanatorium where such things as age and past histories were not important, she would never have noticed him and probably would never have spoken to him, but instead June and Robert, the piano player, who was fifteen years her junior, became inseparable.

When she was stronger and able to leave the hospital, she moved in with Dorothy, where her daughter and now son had been staying. She had rejected Robert's proposal, and upon his release from the hospital, he left Ottawa for Winnipeg. But he returned six months later, asked her again, and she realized then how much she had missed him. At the time June thought the hostility of his family toward her because of their difference in age would be the challenge of their marriage. She never guessed this concern would soon be eclipsed by his next illness and then death. They had two children before he fell ill with liver cancer, and when she was widowed again at forty-four and was left with four children, she found herself poor, truly poor, for the first time in her life.

Before her second husband's death the family had moved into a public housing development on the outskirts of Ottawa and she took a job working in a department store uptown. The streets of the neighbourhood were lined with red brick duplexes and townhouses, divided by laneways where old cars and yard equipment were stashed. She asked that her children be with her for Sunday dinner, and they often, as she and her brothers and sisters had done years before, invited friends to share dinner with them. The table set with china inherited from her mother and silverware from a favourite aunt, she would reminisce during the meal about the dinners on Nelson Street, the way things were when she was a child. As she spoke she remembered autumn evenings when the dining room was lit by candles and the night came in, wrapping their big old house in darkness.

Over the years, June and her sisters stayed in each other's lives, calling weekly when they didn't live in the same city, more frequently when they did. Dorothy, Joseph and their daughter Sophia moved to a small town along the St. Lawrence River and lived in a brick bungalow on a street of similar bungalows, close to a park and water tower. It was a comfortable existence, one that ensured Sophia could attend university and that their routine of shopping and cleaning, meals and watching television, continued with minimum intrusion from the world around them.

In August 1959 Rita left the hospital in the Laurentians, June's second husband had been dead two years and Margaret moved from her house in Aylmer to the outskirts of Rockcliffe Park, where her world was to close in and become the size and shape of her apartment.

One evening in the spring of 1968 when Margaret was sixty-three, she called June and said that someone was outside the building installing wires in her bedroom window for surveillance. "Don't be absurd," June said. "You live on the tenth floor." But Margaret said she could see the men and wires clearly, and if June didn't come over, she was going to call the police. This delusion was the first sign for June that Margaret was ill.

After June calmed Margaret she sat across from the bed watching the restless sleep of her oldest sister. An hour later when June went to the living room to leave, she stood and looked at her sister's apartment, at the expensive furniture, porcelain figurines and crystal in the buffet, items that heightened June's sadness. Her own home stood in stark contrast to the order and quiet of these rooms. She would never have been able to hear the even tick of the clock over the sounds of her house, the radio, telephone conversations and television or the interruptions from her children. In the stillness of her sister's living room she felt that she had rediscovered something precious, long lost, something that had been in the house where she grew up, a slowness akin to the order and custom of her life when she lived with her parents.

The next morning Margaret woke in her bedroom where the sun stretched across the ceiling, bringing with it the full light of a spring day. She had been dreaming about her husbands, alternately waltzing with the two of them in a large ballroom, and as she danced, her memory of the previous night swung back at her. She remembered being terrified by men standing outside her window, by the cavernous hollows of their eyes as they smiled in at her.

In the last year people from her past, people now dead, had begun to visit. First it was only their voices she would hear in other rooms, but gradually she would look up from watching the television and see them in the room across from her, sometimes humming, sometimes watching her and sometimes rambling on about past grievances.

"Philip cheated on you, you know, every chance he got. You couldn't have been that stupid as to not guess." Margaret tried to ignore the voice of a woman who had been a customer in the salon years before, but she continued, accusing Philip of sleeping with neighbours, making passes at June's eldest daughter and stealing money from Margaret. When Margaret accused her visitors of being figments of her imagination, they would sulk back into their chairs until later in the evening, when they would start again. "Look at you," they would say, "the pretty one, the one who got the millionaire; look at you now." *How I wish they'd all shut up*, she would think and turn her thoughts back to the rooms of their house on Nelson Street.

The last day of her life, Margaret woke at eleven in the morning. Her throat felt sore, her tongue coated. She went into the bathroom to wash, stopped and looked at her eyes, which had in the past been bright but now appeared filmed and dull. She brushed her teeth and then went into the kitchen to make coffee. She could see her living room and balcony beyond; she could see rain falling, and the grey light that settled on the room, like dust. She turned on the television and sat with her coffee. "So, Meg, what do you think this all means?" Philip asked her. She glanced from the television and saw him sitting in the chair at the other side of the room; he was dressed in a suit with wide lapels, a hat that shadowed his face and shoes made from alligator leather. He looked uncomfortable and out of place.

"You're a damn fool, Philip," she said, turning back to the television. "You know nothing about life now."

"Then I must know less," Bradley said from the dining room. "Why didn't you ever tell me that you didn't love me? Why did you let me think all those years that there was something wrong with me?"

He seemed slighter than she remembered and wore pajamas, slippers and a satin dressing gown with his initials embroidered on the pocket. "Why are you two ganging up on me?" she asked before she got up and left the living room. In the bedroom her mother sat in the corner in a chair upholstered in the same floral fabric as her curtains and bedspread. "You were always the clever one, Margaret, the one who was going to go somewhere."

"Ghosts," Margaret muttered. "My life is jammed with ghosts." She got back into bed and fell asleep to the sounds of her husbands in the living room. At three in the afternoon, with the curtains closed against the dull day, the ringing phone woke her from a dream where she was back home, lost in an upstairs room. It was Rita speaking about what she was going to make for dinner, about the neighbour she had met in the hallway, her daughter's trip to Florida. Margaret sat up in the bed and took a cigarette from the package on the night table, lighting it. She could still see her mother sitting in the same chair across from her, her face obscured by the room's darkness but her hand on the arm of the chair clearly visible in the light from the window. "That's a good idea, Rita," Margaret said in answer to one of her sister's comments. "How about if I give you a call back when I'm up and more awake." She put the receiver down, continued smoking and looked at her mother. "So, Mother, what's going to happen now?" she said and struggled to lift herself up to get her robe and slippers.

When Margaret did not call back, Rita called her son, who lived close to Margaret and who found her lying on the carpet in her bedroom, face down, her leg turned in at an awkward angle. He called an ambulance, then his mother, who in turn called her sisters. Margaret had hit her head on the dresser, it was confirmed, and had never regained consciousness, but June always thought the reason for the accident was Margaret's growing confusion, the onset of dementia, the ailment that had also struck their mother.

⋈

When Rita called Dorothy it was six o'clock, the evening news had just started, and Dorothy was watching it in the living room with Joseph. She loved the room, decorated with burgundy velvet chairs and floral love seats. She loved that she had chosen the furniture, had spent weeks searching for the material to match the chairs and curtains. She loved the scent of new fabric, which was still discernible and the stiffness of the upholstery when she sat on it. "Now who could that be?" she said. In the last few years her hair had turned white, and it puffed about her head in thick tufts. Her eyes were still pale blue, but rimmed with red, so that she always looked on the verge of crying. "Oh no," she said and sat down slowly into the chair by the telephone, "Who found her?" She spoke in such a hushed voice that Joseph turned and saw her blank stare, the pinch above her eyes that told him something was wrong.

By the time Margaret died, Joseph had retired, and he and Dorothy were ensconced in their life in Kingston, a life of routine where they shopped on certain days, ate the same meal on Sundays and watched the television most nights. And their lives continued like this, with little variation for more than ten years after Margaret's death. But one day in December, when they were both in their mid-seventies, Dorothy went into the spare room and saw Joseph sitting on the end of the bed, crying. The street outside the window was dark with an impending storm. "What's wrong, why are you in here?" Dorothy asked.

"I didn't know where I was. I thought this was my house on Clement but everything looked different."

"Well, it's not, and God knows where you got that idea," she said, but she was worried, not only by his confusion but she too felt at times as if she were in the rooms of her past. A smell in the kitchen or a sound from the street would remind her of the house on Nelson Street, so that all she had to do was close her eyes, and then sometimes even when she opened them she was still there, transfixed in the upstairs hallway or standing in the kitchen, listening to her mother in the pantry. She would not want to return to the present but wished instead to stay and search for her mother, whom she had not realized she missed so deeply.

In the next year Joseph and Dorothy lived an increasingly insular life, seldom visiting anyone, relying only on their failing perceptions to make sense of their days. Gradually they came to distrust even these, withdrawing from each other, until one night Joseph did not recognize Dorothy sitting up in bed watching the television. He came into the room and demanded, "What have you done to my wife?" and Dorothy, not understanding the question, or his distress, shooed him from the bedroom where she stayed, the television blaring. In search of his wife Joseph drove, still dressed in his pajamas, to the shopping mall close to their home. There he walked the halls until someone called the police who brought him to the hospital.

A few weeks later it was also necessary to hospitalize Dorothy, when she broke her hip in a fall. Their daughter Sophia arrived from England where she had been living, and was alarmed when Dorothy at times did not recognize her and when her father said words she could not understand. Dorothy would lie in bed looking out the window, sometimes silent, sometimes talking about her girlhood on Nelson Street—Sunday dinners when the dining room was crowded with family and friends all talking at the same time, or she would hear the sound of taffeta gowns on the day Margaret was married and June laughing as they rushed down the stairway. When her daughter would leave Dorothy's room, the memories crowded in again and she would be alone with the slow process of her death. When she did die some months later, Sophia was there beside her. Minutes before, when she had to cough, Dorothy put her hand up to her mouth, the last movement in her life a gesture of courtesy, of decorum.

Rita died the same year as her sister Dorothy. For many years she stayed in the apartment building where she had moved after her divorce. After earning his PhD in history, her youngest son moved away to live with a woman Rita could not understand. This woman wore heavy black glasses, her short hair cut in a severe style and she had a habit of looking just to the left of Rita's eyes when she spoke. Often she would accompany Rita's son when he came for Sunday night dinner and they would spend the meal discussing world affairs, complaining about dictatorships and fascism, excluding Rita who smiled and busied herself with the meal or tidying up after.

Through those years whenever her children spoke of their father, Rita felt a heaviness in her chest and was compelled to ask questions. *How was he surviving without me?* was really what she wanted to ask, but in order to counter the look of discomfort she saw on her children's faces, she learnt to temper her questions to simple enquires about his health, or new residence. Her children said she never really got over his leaving, that it was the pivot upon which all her disappointments revolved, but more and more it seemed to Rita as if her marriage was a story that had not ended, a mystery that remained unresolved.

When she had a bad fall in her early 80s, her daughter arranged for her to move to a retirement home; there she became increasingly quiet and disoriented and by the time of her death she had moved again to a nursing home where she lived for the last five years of her life. By the time of her death she was on the top floor, where patients stayed who never went out and needed constant attention. Her sister June used to visit and they would sit in the sunroom near the nurses' station. At first, during these visits, they would discuss their children or their own childhoods, but as the years went on Rita usually only answered her sister's questions with a smile. Often there was nothing to say, and so June would style Rita's hair, standing behind her delivering a running monologue. "Remember how we used to do this at home and father would get so angry about the hair in the sink?" Combing her sister's hair, now a pale grey, she would ask "What do you think?" handing Rita a compact mirror. But Rita only smiled up at her without speaking, with a look of soft compliance.

June often told her children the story of her father's death when he was ninety-five. He had lived in Tallahassee with his third wife, a woman of sixty-nine, and the story went that he had walked on the beach and eaten a meal of lobster and crab at a restaurant the night before he was brought to the hospital. He suffered a heart attack and was gone within the day. June would tell this story to her youngest daughter, Amy, and then say how she hoped her children inherited his genes.

But it was June who was blessed with her father's genes, living into her nineties, still in her own apartment, still reading the newspaper every morning, visiting with her children and speaking to Amy most days. If Amy wanted to please her, she would ask her about her life on Nelson Street, and June would tell her about the clatter from the horses and buggies, the way the street looked in the afternoon when her mother would not allow her and her younger brother off the veranda, or how the high windows in the living room would be left open all night to catch the summer breeze. She would tell stories about her sisters, describing the years when they were young, helping their mother with the dinner and cleaning, working at the Chateau Laurier in their teens and later visiting Margaret at her riverfront home. Amy had heard these stories before, she knew her aunts, had witnessed their lives and was often bored or noncommittal when her mother would begin her recollections. But Amy also knew when her mother spoke of her home how fond her memories were and how she had tried to create the same kind of solid place for her children. Often now as she was nearing the end of her life, when June spoke of her sisters and the years they lived together, a softness would come over her face, a contemplation, the look that let Amy know she was really talking about love.

AURA

Amy entered her parents' bedroom in the late afternoon gloom of a winter day. She watched her father sleeping. A crucifix hung on the wall above him, with a dried palm from the previous Easter draped over it. Four years old, she had climbed the staircase to see him, after hearing her mother and sister talking about his illness, how he would probably go to the hospital and there was no guarantee what would happen to him there. The room was hot and moist. The sound of her family, watching television or talking with the radio on, was faintly heard in this room filled with the sound of her father's shallow breathing.

She approached the bed. Barefoot and dressed in a nightgown, she could feel the floorboards under her feet, as frost in a crystal pattern vined its way across the window pane. By his side she looked at his face closed in sleep. There was a glass of water and books on the night table, and on the bed beside him lay the rosary he used every night so that if she would wake it was to the muffled sound of his praying, bead by bead. His eyes opened, flickered and shut, as he retreated to somewhere familiar, the bedroom of his own childhood perhaps, to a dusk like this dusk, when the wind blew cold and he could see the line of light under the door of his parents' room. Or a spring day with his mother in the front seat of their car, when she turned her head, lifted her hand to her mouth after a sharp laugh, and looked back to the knitting in her lap. *What was she making*, he wondered. It had been a long time since he had seen her this young, and when he looked closely, he realized her auburn hair and hazel eyes made her a pretty woman. In this memory—with the sun beating into the car creating patches of light and dark—he leaned against the backseat window watching the familiar streets of white-trimmed brick houses slide past.

In other moments when the pain subsided—a pain that bloomed so fiercely he was forced to curl around it—he succumbed to the memory of his family during a late summer dinner with his mother at one end of the table, his father at the other. His sisters were across from him, and the baby, his brother, in a high chair beside him. They ate slowly in the heat.

"Mother, I'm going to be in the school concert," his oldest sister said. The baby looked at her, his eyes wide and deep blue. His mother fed the child with a constant movement from the bowl to his small open mouth, any dribble caught by the spoon.

He slapped the tray of his high chair with an open hand and his mother said, "Be a good boy, no hitting." They were eating pork chops, fresh beans and mashed potatoes. A basket of bread sat on the table, glasses of milk in front of the children. "What, dear? You'll be in a play. Well, that's wonderful."

Nothing out of the ordinary, this dinner, and yet he often found himself sitting there, his feet not touching the floor, his arms too short to reach the bread basket. The year was 1940, when he was ten years old. Outside a storm approached; the room darkened and thunder rumbled around them as wind, caught in the yard, stirred the air. A branch slapped the back window and his father said, "I must cut that tree, remind me when the weather is better."

Years later, during a day in early May, he and his mother visited his oldest sister in the hospital after she gave birth to her first child. His mother wore a pillbox hat with a matching veil, a mauve tailored suit and low-heeled shoes the same colour. She looked through the glass at the babies in a line of basinets before the window. "Look at her," his sister said, "look at her little face." The baby's face was puffy and blotched and her tiny hands curled by her head were like unopened buds. His mother tilted her head and said, "Yes, she looks like Sally when she was a baby, but I'd ask the doctors about that rash, that's not normal." He heard these words again as if his mother was in the room with him. Had the day really happened like that? His sister and mother with him in the hallway, whispering until his mother's comment, when they stood silently staring in at the row of swaddled babies.

In his uneasy sleep the father returned to the grounds of the sanatorium where he had been confined for TB at the age of eighteen and where he met the woman who would be his wife, the mother of their two children. She was older, widowed, and already had a son and daughter from a first marriage. Now when he would wake feverish, it was her hand he felt resting on his forehead and her care that kept him comfortable, or as comfortable as possible in the widening landscape of his pain. By the early 1950s they had moved from an apartment in New Edinburgh to the house where his son and daughter would grow up, to those yards scribbled with clotheslines and electrical wires and the moving tangles of dogs and children. It was here in the last cold days of 1956, as he slept in an upstairs bedroom, that his daughter came into the room in early evening, and watched the shadows settle in the creases of the blankets, the way mist seen from a high vantage rests in the hollows of valleys and fields.

A simple cross above the door, his hands upon the sheets, thin and pale, his rosary in a jumble beside a water glass on the bedside table, the heat, the dull light of dusk filtering into the room, and the young girl standing by the bedside looking at her father. It would be this moment with its distance and their separate solitudes that stays with her. The static room where he lay recalling his life in fragments was the place she moved away from into the rest of her life. The moment came back when she heard the sadness in a violin's single, elongated note, when a painting touched her with its precise gradient of colour, the rose blush of a bashful cheek or when a still scene appeared before her: a street made black from soft rain, the expanse of the ocean behind the long stretch of beach, snow falling silently before a window. These things of beauty would link her to the moment with her father, when his resting body seemed to glow with a pale aura. His life ended two months later, on a cold, sunny February day in a hospital room; the scenes of his life closed in on him, stopped; his wife and parents standing around the bed, his children half a city away.

HER MOTHER'S DAUGHTER

Before the mirror my mother arranged the mesh veil of her hat, rubbed her front tooth to erase a smear of red lipstick, and turned her head from side to side to view herself from all angles. It was a Saturday morning in early December 1957 and she was preparing to visit her sister, Margaret, in Montreal in order to attend the wedding of a childhood friend. Sitting in front of the vanity with its triptych of mirrors and assortment of creams and makeup, my mother hummed, tried on different necklaces, and spoke to me about the wedding, the reception, and how she was looking forward to seeing the bride's gown. We could hear my brother, two years older than me, in the bedroom across the hall, issuing commands to his toy soldiers and making sounds for the explosions. Out the window snow began to fall, the beginning of a storm that would last all weekend. My mother had arranged for my brother and me to stay with our grandparents while she was away. Our father, their son, had died the previous winter and she said it was important that we spend time with them. But I would have preferred to be with my brother and sister, teenagers, the children from my mother's first marriage, who were allowed to stay at home.

That winter, the year I turned five, my mother had begun work as a hostess in an evening club called The Red Door. It showcased singers and orchestras and served steaks and fries to patrons who sat at round tables near the stage. She brought home paper umbrellas for me, the type used to make drinks look festive and I kept them for years, until the paper tore. During this season when it snowed on the duplexes and townhouses where we lived on the outskirts of Ottawa, we were all in our separate ways coming to terms with the deepening meaning of the loss of my father. Winter suited us: the howl of wind, the frost as thick as calluses on the window, the sleet we could see blowing along the icy sidewalks in long, crystal strands, all served to isolate us in our home that creaked under the weight of all that winter snow.

My grandparents' red brick house had white trim and a back yard outlined by spruce and cedar hedges, a yard I remember best in the blue light of a winter afternoon. Nearby streets, parks and school grounds made up a neighbourhood built after the Second World War for civil servants and working class families. They're there still, those houses, like old women hunched over knitting or mending or some task that forced their concentration inward.

I watched my mother leave from the living room window of my grandparents' house after she dropped us off and spoke to my grandmother in the closed vestibule. Moving into the street, her small form black against the white snow, she turned before entering the car and looked back at the house, frowned and cupped her hand over her eyes as if searching for something against the glare. Years later she confided, "Before I left I had this panicky feeling that I should go back and take you with me, and I always wished I had."

"Okay, kids, I don't want you making a mess," my grandmother said. "So go in the basement and watch TV." Then she called to my grandfather, "Harry, put the television on for the kids." The order of her house was a direct result of her unflinching will, her unrelenting routine of scouring, scrubbing, and polishing, and her belief that the uncertainties of life could be tamed by these activities. On her knees with a bucket of hot water before her, she'd wring out the cloth to scrub the floors and walls, a mist steaming from her hands as if they were blessed objects, and surely this was how she saw her quest: divinely ordained, moral in import.

It was the custom that during dinners only my grandparents spoke, usually about the neighbours, the price of food or their other grandchildren. "When Monica was here last week, she was wearing such a smart coat, with ermine trim." Monica was my cousin, the only child of my father's sister. "She's clever, that one. She's reading her father's books now, and she loves that show, the educational one, have you ever heard it, Amy? No, probably not." Although repetitive, my grandmother's conversations often filled me with anxiety for I never knew when she'd call on me to comment, which she did that night, "Amy, when did your mother say she'd pick you up?"

"Tomorrow, grandmother, after lunch." We were eating rare roast beef, and I was having difficulty swallowing. A pale smear of pink remained on my plate.

"So. She thinks she can…" she said, looking at my grandfather. When he did not respond she stopped speaking. The sound of cutlery on plates, my grandfather's dull cough, the radiator's hiss, filled the silence until she said, "So, I suppose we'll have to put the Christmas decorations up soon."

"Yes, I suppose," my grandfather responded simply. He was a compact man with neatly combed grey hair, who wore a white shirt, suit and bow tie to his job at an insurance company during the week, and a cardigan or vest on the weekends.

My grandmother said, "Amy, I'd wish you stop swinging your legs under the table. Young ladies don't do that." She was holding her knife and fork in her hands, her wrists braced by the table edge, her face drained of colour, and her eyes, when I dared to look, were dark points of anger.

My brother looked back and forth between the two of us until my grandmother turned her attention to him and said, "And you, mister, you should be sitting quiet too. God knows where you get your manners." Yet I knew she did not expect conflict from him; all serious matters, the only kind of power important to her, were elements that involved women in the family. Her dealings with him—perhaps because he looked and acted like my father at that age—and even her tone as she chastised him was often comic, as if he were a dog, unruly and innocent.

⚜

My grandmother was sitting up in bed, her feet, twin points under the blankets, a net over her head covering pin curlers, like rows of tiny artillery. On my way back from the washroom I could see them from the hallway—my grandfather reading, my grandmother putting cream on her elbows. "Did you turn the light off?" she asked when she saw me and when I responded she said, "Good. Now get some sleep." Well into the night, from the room where my brother and I lay, I could hear them, as cars passing before the house created wide arcs of moving light on the ceiling. I knew they were speaking about my mother because her name was the only word I could make out.

The next morning, from the large picture window in the living room, we could see snow falling so thick it was difficult to make out the neighbours across the street decorating their house with Christmas lights. My mother, caught in Montreal by the snowstorm, called to say she might not be back until after dinner. After the call, my grandmother put down the receiver. "Well, that's just typical," she said to my grandfather. "For one thing there's not enough room at the dining room table." My aunt, uncle and cousin were coming for their customary Sunday dinner. "So the kids will have to eat in the kitchen. And I hate making a mess in two rooms."

⚜

Later in the day, my grandmother stood by the front door as snow continued to fall, welcoming my aunt and her family, "Come in, come in. It's just awful out there." When they entered the front hall she added, "Joe, you can put your galoshes here," pointing to a plastic mat she had cleaned and put in the hallway. "The TV is on downstairs everyone," she said to my uncle and me and to then to Monica: "Why don't you go and watch it with your Grandpa?"

"Good idea," my uncle said and went through the kitchen to the stairs that led to the rec room.

My grandmother moved to the stove and shook salt into a large pot of vegetable soup while I stood in the kitchen doorway, Monica beside me. My aunt and grandmother busied themselves with the dinner, with their backs to us. Standing like this they looked remarkably similar, two thin straight women, the same height with aprons tied in bows at their waists.

"Well I had it out," my grandmother said. "I just told her."

"What did you say?" my aunt asked.

"I told her it wasn't right with two young kids to work where she does, to see those men she sees. I just told her to remember she shares my last name. Do you know what she said? She said, 'I'm going to live my own life.' How could she be like that?" The steam from the pot created a mist on the window. "I was right, wasn't I, to say something, I mean?"

"You have to do what feels right, Mom," my aunt said.

I watched a car creep by on the street. My grandmother said, "And now she leaves them here with me because she's stuck in some snowstorm and I'm just supposed to feed and look after them. And God knows what she's really doing." She stopped chopping and put her hand on her hip. "Besides, I think living with her has perverted them, especially Amy." I moved around into the hallway where she could not see me, but where I could still see the window. "Just before you came, I caught her up in the attic eavesdropping over the grill. Listening to us. She's become a moody little thing, really, her mother's daughter."

Monica went to her grandmother's side, "When's dinner, Grandma?"

"Well, my, look who's here." My grandmother bent down to hug her before saying, "Such a good girl." Out the steamy window I could see Christmas lights that snaked around the windows and doors of the houses across the street, smeared red, yellow, and green circles.

)(

That afternoon my brother and I had been told to stay in the rec room. The thought made me itchy and so instead, when I knew my grandmother was busy, I went to the attic. There I knew I could sit alone in front of the dormer window, watching the snow and listening to the house beneath me. The room was disorganized and I liked not having to listen or care; that I could let the sounds of their voices simply drift up and dissipate into the attic's cool air.

I fell asleep and an hour later woke to my grandmother mounting the steps. When she saw me, she said, "When I call you, you come. Do you understand?" She was wearing a white blouse and grey skirt, pearls around her neck, hands on her hips. Her apron was patterned with daisies and bluebells. I remembered this detail because I was staring at the fabric rather than looking at her face. There had been times when I'd sensed her anger, but it had never been so close before. Her shoes, black and laced, made a chafing noise on the floor, as she pushed me in front of her toward the stairs, and there was a kitchen smell emanating from her, warm and yeasty. "What's the attraction up here anyway?" She stopped and we could hear classical music playing from the den and my grandfather's cough. "So that's it. You were listening to us, like a little sneak. Listening to us so that... What? You could tell her?" She hurried me down the stairs and at the bottom turned to face me and spat the words: "You are just like her." There it was. The truth, as she knew it, the truth we were locked on either side of.

It seemed an immeasurable amount of time that we stood like this, her face close to mine, her eyes dark with anger and I wonder what forced time to resume. The sound of a door shutting perhaps, a car in the lane way or the bark of a neighbour's dog, these sounds crept into the moment, but what stayed was the intensity of her expression. Antagonism and then derision gathered there, freezing for a terrible instant, receding gradually and leaving finally an uncompromising inaccessibility and I felt, not for the last time, that sense of childhood hopelessness and entrapment.

After my grandfather's death when I was in my early twenties, my grandmother stayed alone in the house where they had lived for more than forty years. I'd think of her there, imagine the rooms closing in. The winter veils of snow moving across the yard, the neighbourhood children coming home in the mauve light of four o'clock—she must have seen all this from the window in the kitchen that looked out onto the street. That same window where in 1957 I saw the smudged orbs of colour from the Christmas lights. What would she think standing alone by that window, the rooms of the house she knew so well behind her, clean and silent?

On a winter day, ten years after my grandfather's death, my grandmother died. My mother called to tell me that my aunt had found her at the bottom of the basement stairs when she'd gone to pick her up for Sunday dinner. She'd been dead several hours.

I see her lying there so clearly, it is as if I'm there. It's as if in my heart I'm there as a child, sitting in that room, not moving, being quiet, my hands in my lap. I look at her; the tangle of her eighty-five-year-old body, a knot that cannot be untied. Snow piles against the basement window making it difficult to see the yard or the light. I can hear the wind's howl breaking the winter silence. And in a fierce revelation I finally understand the merciless power of youth and patience.

FIRST SNOW

When my marriage was first failing and I would try to understand what it meant for the future, I'd think back to my aunt Rita's house on the evening my uncle told his family he was leaving. I had not been there that night, but I heard my mother and aunt speaking the following day and I remembered it had snowed, the first snow of 1958, the year I was six. I had always loved my aunt's home, a large stone house on a street where other large brick and stone houses stood divided by arbours and laneways. I knew how her living room would have looked on that November evening, with its furniture caught in the light of dusk, mirrors along the wall, and the set of double doors that opened onto a patio.

In my imagining of that night, my cousin Claire is my age and sitting on the yellow floral chesterfield, she wore a blue dress covered by an embroidered white smock with a ruffled slip of eyelet beneath, the kind of dress a heroine in a children's story might wear, the kind of dress I would have loved to own. Her shoes were black patent leather and her ankle socks bright white and rimmed with lace. She was the beating heart in that immaculate room of high ceilings and satin curtains, precious with youth although her face was flushed from crying. When a door closed upstairs, she stopped, straightened and listened, looking toward the sound. Tears sat on her smooth cheeks like dew.

At the sound of someone descending the stairs, Claire wiped her tears away and waited. As the night filled the room, so had an atmosphere of secrecy, of a complicated silence. She leaned over and snapped on the table lamp beside her. It was a quick sound, a period at the end of a sentence. My uncle appeared at the door, dressed in a large brown coat and fedora. His unhappy face hung like a heavy sack. "Claire," he said.

"Yes, Daddy." The light made all the difference for the room now seemed sunny, the glass of the coffee table gleamed and the mirrors reflected the room crisply, giving a sense of clean, limitless space.

"Everything is going to be okay," he said. "I've spoken with your mother." He was in the room now, not far from his daughter who had tucked her legs beneath her. "Yes, Daddy," she said again. Outside long scarves of loose night drifted down pathways, caught on hedges, and tangled in the dead flowers and weeds of their garden.

The silence was broken by the sound of a radio coming from the upstairs bedroom of her brothers, Jim and Glen. Their joint room was on the first landing; it was large with a bed on either side, a basketball hoop behind the door, clothes on the floor, books, papers scattered on the dressers and their shared desk. Jim had pronounced features, heavy eyebrows, and a stubborn cowlick in his dark hair while Glen was fair with blue eyes, his hairline already receding. Glen squinted from the effort of tossing a basketball in the air with one hand. It made him look angry. The radio on low played Elvis Presley, "Love Me Tender." At thirteen, Jim, younger by three years, stood before his brother. "It means we will probably have to move, that's what it means," he said. They were dressed similarly, in corduroy pants and ski sweaters; Glen's tied in a knot around his neck. "Well, so," he said, "We'll be okay."

"What if they ask us to choose?" Jim said.

Glen stopped tossing the ball and sat up. "They wouldn't ask us to do that." He did not want to be part of this dilemma, this family. The day before he'd met a girl, someone new at school, and now nothing was as real to him as her face, her clear blue eyes, the feeling he had as he walked away. Even as he spoke to his brother he was thinking of the way her hair was drawn back and how her smile made him swell with anticipation, almost happiness.

My aunt opened the door. "Boys?" Her presence was unassuming but her voice spiked with worry. *This is a stupid waste of time*, Glen thought and began to toss the ball higher as Jim turned sadly to look at her.

My aunt was a small woman, gentle and easily flustered. She was wearing a gold satin dressing gown that matched the blonde hair piled on her head; soft curls fell about her neck. She moved as if in a trance. "Boys," she said again, "I don't want you to worry, I..." she stumbled a little into the room, sat on the edge of Glen's bed and moved her hand to her cheek. "I," she raised her head. "I mean, we'll be fine, one way or the other."

Neither boy spoke as she stood and left the room. She moved slowly, lifting her dressing gown and as she walked, the sound of heavy fabric dragging on carpet followed her. Her bedroom was cream and gold and behind the bed's quilted satin headboard was a wall of mirrored tiles. She stopped when she entered the room and looked at herself in the mirror. Just a few minutes before, her husband had stood where she was standing, as she had looked out the window and let his words sink into her. Even as he spoke, part of her was detached, watching the night move over the street.

Her arms hung motionless by her side, her head tilted, as if she were straining to hear distant voices, her pain so pure it was a stillness that reached out and settled into the room. How could she know there would be days in the future when she would again be content, when she'd arrange flowers and make meals and sit with her son watching television? She heard Glen and Jim speaking over the sound of Glen's basketball and she wondered if Claire had spoken with her father before he left.

※

In my imagining I leave her here and move to the attic, my favourite room of their old house. At the top of the stairs hung a cord that turned on a light bulb when tugged. It swung for a moment like a loose eye, forcing the shadows of boxes, garment bags and furniture to sway about the room. Past the clutter, out the dormer window that looked down at the front of the house, snow fell on cars in laneways and on the street, collecting on windowsills and in doorways.

On the path that led from the front door, my uncle stopped and turned back to look at the house. His face was hidden, lost in the shadow of his fedora, arms loose by his side. He stood like this long enough for snow to gather thick on the rim of his hat. Then he closed the top button of his coat and pulled the scarf tight around his neck. *He wants to be someone different,* I thought. *He wants to start over.* It was such a simple wish that looking down on him even I could feel it.

When my uncle was gone, snow filled the sidewalk where he'd stood; only a sense of absence remained. The house below lay quiet. My thoughts from this evening stall here, in the attic, where I stand wondering if my aunt and cousins are now sleeping; if they, each in their own way, have returned to their separate worlds. The snow is thinning; a few lost flakes wander before the window. Soon the evening's final darkness will consume the view and I will be left standing by the window looking out at the cold sky, and it will appear to me, not for the last time, like the future descending.

THE WEDDING

Amy stood on the steps of the church, holding a bouquet of assorted flowers: pink carnations, gardenias and baby's breath, a bouquet her mother had made that morning with twine and white ribbons. Seven years old, she was to be the flower girl in her sister Natalie's wedding and had been sent ahead to the church with her uncle Joe, aunt Dorothy and Claire, a cousin and the daughter of her aunt Rita. Rita with her two sons, Jim and Glen, were already on the grounds of the church when Joe drove his lumbering Plymouth into the gravel parking lot. On the top step of the wide staircase Amy stood by the two large doors that when opened gave her a view of the vestry and nave, a billowing dark space smelling of wood polish and incense. But mostly she watched the crowd on the lawn and pathway —friends and relatives mixing with those of the groom, Johnny.

Earlier, as maid of honour, Claire had gone to the bride's house to be photographed with the bridal party before the wedding. Now at the church, she looked perfectly photogenic. Tall and blonde, she wore a purple lace dress that gathered at her waist and flared to just below her knee; on her feet, satin high heels with pointed toes, dyed the same colour as her gown. Now, from the top step by the church doors, Amy watched her aunt Dorothy pin a wide brimmed hat on Claire, her expression intent as she held pins in her mouth and spoke rapidly around them. "You'll still have to hold it in the wind—this is really just a lick and a promise."

Amy looked past Claire and Dorothy to the far end of the pathway from where her aunt Margaret with her uncle Phil approached. *There she is,* Amy thought; the last time Amy had seen her aunt the week before she'd promised to buy Amy the bride and groom ornament that she'd seen in a photograph of the bridal cake. Margaret and her husband were walking arm in arm, her other hand holding her coat shut, and Amy worried because she could not see the dolls (as she thought of them) or any place they could be hidden. She rushed down the steps. "Where's my bride and groom?" she asked without preamble. But Dorothy had seen Margaret too and was asking her sister about the outfit she was wearing.

"What?" Margaret said in a distracted way, unhooking her arm from her husband and bending slightly to speak with Amy, but then immediately straightening to answer Dorothy. "Oh no, I decided to wear this instead."

"My dolls!" Amy said.

"Your dolls?" Margaret echoed. "My, don't you look sweet." She turned to Dorothy, "Doesn't she look sweet? The prettiest little girl, don't you think Dorothy?"

"Oh, yes, the dress's cute," Dorothy responded. "But June and Natalie kept her up all night finishing it and I think she's a little crabby."

I am not, Amy thought. "The dolls, Aunt Margaret, you promised."

"What is it sweetie? What dolls?" Margaret turned to Claire who was standing beside Dorothy, "That's a beautiful dress, Claire, very attractive."

"Thanks, I like it too," Claire said.

Amy's voice rose, "But you told me, you said you'd get them for me."

"I don't know what you're talking about, Amy," Margaret stood straight and looked down as she spoke. "What dolls?"

"On the cake. You promised."

"Oh, the ornaments." Margaret arched her back as if she was about to laugh at the thought. "Well, not today, today's the wedding." She waved to her nephew Jim. "You have a job today Amy. You can't play with dolls. Besides aren't you getting too old for that?"

)(

At that very moment the bride was alone in the upstairs washroom of her home; she was dressed in a slip having removed her wedding dress after the photographer and the bridal party had left. She applied lipstick and eyeliner for the sixth time that day. "What are you doing in there?" her mother, June, said from the hallway.

June was the youngest amongst the sisters Dorothy, Rita and Margaret. She was widowed twice, the first time when the father of Natalie and Lawrence died, and then again when the father of Amy and Amy's brother Stevie died. A small woman with dark hair styled in a pageboy, she usually wore heels and dressed most often in black and white, although on the day of the wedding she wore a dark blue suit with a pencil skirt and a tight fitting pill box hat.

Before her second husband died the family moved to a duplex, part of a housing development in a new subdivision in the east end of the city, and after his death she'd began work as the hostess at a dinner club. When she proved herself, she was put in charge of the club's finances and helped with booking the orchestras and singing acts. She became a favourite of the owner, a wizened man with a past that included numerous indiscretions, and, as a thank you, he'd offered the downstairs convention room for Natalie's wedding reception.

"We need to leave shortly," June said through the door. Natalie looked at herself in the mirror, and instantly felt the division between who she was, what she felt, and the image in front of her. In the dream she'd had only a few hours earlier she was also looking at herself in a mirror when she saw a white pimple on her forehead. Oh no, she thought, not today. And she pinched it but it kept issuing a white paste-like substance in a cord, like a tiny toothpaste coil, while she, now frantic, thought, this can't be happening. In the future when she'd see her wedding photographs, despite the smiles, the manicured appearance and the posed attractiveness of the wedding group, what she remembered was that white coil that would not stop oozing. Decades later when she told Amy, she laughed and said it was like all the horribleness imaginable had found a portal into the world.

Natalie's memory of that October wedding day in 1959 was a mixture of intense awareness and yet, inexplicably, forgetfulness, as if the event had been so vivid that her over-saturated mind could not grasp it in any normal way. She could only liken it to a moment of cohesion so profound it seemed that who she'd been in childhood, who she was and who she would become, coalesced. "When I think back all I remember clearly is seeing those people," she said to Amy. "All the important people in my life, gathered together for the day."

"Natalie," her mother said, "Your uncle Joe will be back any minute to pick us up." And Natalie put away the thoughts of the dream as definitively as she put away her lipstick and mascara. She slipped the dress on, opened the door so her mother could help her with the zipper, combed her bangs once more, and was downstairs waiting for her uncle when he returned.

※

Amy went back to standing beside her oldest brother Lawrence on the steps, but she kept her head down, reeling at the unfairness of it all. *Now what will I do for fun*, she wondered. *Just this stupid wedding and then we can't even go home after.* When she looked up she saw the crowd gathering in groups on the lawn and pathways leading from the street and parking lot. She lifted her head and glared at her three aunts who were standing close to each other: her aunt Rita, a blonde, petite woman, animated with talk, her aunt Margaret, the oldest, most flamboyant, and Amy thought, most untrustworthy, in a mink-trimmed suit and a close, veiled hat. Dorothy, the tallest, most maternal, the most serious, turned from her sisters, holding her hat, when the wind rushed at them. Beside Amy, Lawrence, at sixteen, bounced slightly from foot to foot with nervous energy. Her other brother Stephen, who was eight, ran between the grass and steps until Dorothy grabbed him and told him he'd have to calm down.

Amy saw her cousins scattered throughout the crowd. Claire stood with the bridesmaids, smoking, her exhaled smoke aimed high over their heads. Close by, Dorothy's daughter Sophia was in the group with Amy's cousins, Jim and Glen, standing by their sports car. The car was bought by Jim and Glen's father shortly before he left their mother, Rita, to move in with a woman who worked with him. A loud bark of laughter came from the group of ushers standing with the groom, their dark suits and jittery manner giving them the appearance of a gathering of crows.

Before the church a line of oak and maple trees lined the curb, in turn yellow, orange, and red: a bracelet of autumn colour. When the wind blew, in near unison the women put their hands to their heads to hold their hats as the leaves loosened, some falling to the street, on the lawn, and in the ditch along the road. After just such a rush of wind Amy saw her grandmother, her father's mother, arrive in a black Dodge driven by her grandfather, a short man with cropped grey hair, steel-rimmed glasses and yet despite the severity of his appearance his eyes often squinted with amusement. They moved slowly from the car, stopping by the edge of the lawn and stood together.

"Beautiful bright day," Amy's grandfather said but her grandmother hated when such bland statements were used as a way to ward off awkwardness or boredom, and so did not respond. Instead she looked around and realized she did not know most of the people who stood by the sidewalk or in the parking lot. But she did recognize two women, sisters of her daughter-in-law, and when one of them saw her and waved, she smiled weakly and raised her hand.

"Why are the doors not open?" she said, flicking a piece of lint from her skirt. "They ask us to be here by a certain time and then the doors are closed."

"When we first arrived, I saw someone go in," the grandfather said. "It's just everyone seems to be enjoying the day out here."

Amy saw her grandmother speaking to her grandfather and recognized the look of annoyance on her face. The look frightened her and made her momentarily forget her Aunt Margaret's betrayal. Her grandmother often wore this expression when she'd bend to look at Amy, holding the child's elbows tightly, bending down toward her face while Amy noticed the fine circuits of lines around her eyes and lips.

It would take a long time for her view of her grandmother to soften, for Amy to realize her grandmother must have always carried the tragedy of her son's death, almost two years earlier and perhaps it was the search for something of him that made her appraisal of Amy so intense. But on the day of the wedding, standing with her husband, suffering the dull beginning of a headache, Amy's grandmother turned and saw her granddaughter by the front steps and as she did the sun broke out from behind a cloud. The air became clearer and sharper with the autumn colour of the street, the trees, the people and cars now illuminated, and in that instant, without warning, as the sharp light fell from a high distance, she felt again the spear from the loss of her son.

※

As the wealthiest of the sisters, Margaret always wore the most stylish and expensive clothes; she was childless by choice, unlike her sister Dorothy and even though she was fond of Natalie, she was not interested in being part of the chaos of the bridal party. She viewed the fuss over gowns, shoes and makeup as mere commotion. She did admire, though, the end result, the beauty of the bride; it was a currency she appreciated; that and the appearance of the guests, *all gussied up*, as she called it, were things she found worthy of notice.

When Margaret saw June's mother-in-law and waved a greeting, to which she received the slightest of acknowledgements, she said, "I'll be glad to see that bar at the reception," to her husband Phil, himself an avid drinker. The night before, lying quietly beside him, she'd woken to his heavy breathing that escalated to snores and wondered how she'd ended up there, with a man who annoyed as often as amused her.

"What do you mean?" he said.

"I mean I'm feeling whiskey will be in order very soon." She turned then and saw Amy who was looking down from the steps and listening, "You didn't hear that, kid," she said.

Amy usually liked the way her aunt spoke to her, liked that the register of her voice was the same as when she was speaking to any adult, and that she never apologized for swearing, but on this day she was still harboring her grudge. So when her aunt Dorothy walked toward them and said, "Didn't hear what?" Amy answered, "Auntie Margaret wants to see that bar at the reception."

"What did I just tell you?" Margaret said to Amy but she was smiling.

"I think you can wait for a drink Maggie," Dorothy said, her voice rising.

"Of course I can," Margaret said. "I just would rather not." She was amused by her sister, by the way Dorothy straightened and refused to look at her, *mounting her high horse*, as Margaret referred to it.

"Oh for God's sake, Margaret," Dorothy said. Often the sisters' conversations with each other ended with this type of dismissive comment; it was a mark of the honesty, affection and the deep-rooted exasperation of their interactions. Dorothy turned toward the bridesmaids who had gathered at the end of the path, talking and laughing with the ushers.

Oh no, there they go, Rita thought when she heard the tone of Dorothy's voice and turned to see her sisters standing on the lower steps. Closer to the road, the photographer was taking photos of the bridesmaids, asking them to walk along the path, holding their bouquets. He was dressed in a worn suit, shiny at the knees and elbows, frayed at the cuffs; a suit that looked like a costume used many times when he was called upon to play the role of photographer. He had a cigarette dangling from his lips, long fingers of ash falling as he worked. Rita watched and said aloud, "He's going to drop ash on Claire's gown."

Claire looked toward her mother and gave a small wave before the photographer instructed her to look serious. "But be happy too," his cigarette bouncing with each word. This was the first family gathering Rita had attended without her husband and standing there watching her daughter who looked serene and lovely, she felt constricted by her dress and began to feel hot, even though it was not a hot day. The sky was mottled with clouds and the light kept fluctuating from brilliant to subdued as the sun was obscured and then revealed. Rita's thoughts were cut short by the sharp laughter of the ushers who were standing together, the groom off to the side speaking to his sister, and Rita wondered if the cake, her contribution to the wedding, had been delivered to the reception hall.

Johnny stood with his friends and groomsmen Brad and Gus—boys, now men, he'd known since childhood. He was so thin as to be angular, his hair shiny black in a heavy bump above his face, a duck cut in the back, and his features were narrow and likeable. He and his friends had gone out the night before to a bar in the neighbourhood where they'd grown up, and both Brad and Gus became drunk, but Johnny drank only a beer; he'd never been able to drink when he was excited or nervous.

Like Natalie, he lived with his widowed mother, but she was a different sort of mother than June. She wore loose kimonos made of cotton, with a sweater and a pair of Johnny's socks in the winter. Her hair was wild around her head, like grey cotton candy, and she was older, more acerbic, harbouring—it seemed to Natalie—a whole household of regrets and angers. Her comments on most everything, from what appeared on the television (a device that was on from the moment she woke to the moment she went to bed), her neighbours, and any news she heard were invective, sour, and often deeply humorous. Not liking Johnny's friend Gus, she nicknamed him Pus, and Sue, the woman her brother had married and whom she despised, became Sewer.

When she'd be lounging on the chesterfield and Johnny was sitting beside her, she'd poke him with her big toe if she wanted something. "Go get that bag of potato chips in the kitchen," she'd say jabbing him with her pointed foot.

"Christ, Mom, can you keep that hoof away from me."

"This is the thanks I get," and then she'd list everything she'd done for him, starting with giving birth. And yet he knew now that this was not true. She had not given birth to him. He was the result of a relationship between a travelling musician and the girl Johnny had always believed to be his oldest sister. He discovered this not by unearthing some secret correspondence or overhearing talk he was not meant to hear, but he discovered this fact because his sister wanted to be at the head table with the groom and bride.

A few days before the wedding, Natalie went with Johnny to explain to his mother what would happen on the day of their marriage. His sister Sandy arrived in the apartment shortly after them, and Johnny could tell she'd been drinking and that the evening would most probably end with his mother and sister arguing. As he spoke to his mother she grunted and tried to look beyond him and Natalie to the television until he turned the set off. "Come on, Mom. We want you to be part of this."

"Yeah, well," his mother said and before she could say more Sandy, who'd been standing in the doorway, a beer bottle in her hand, said, "It really should be me up there."

"Where?" Johnny said. "You don't even know what we're talking about."

"Oh yes, I do, and you don't know what I'm talking about."

Natalie was used to Sandy's talk and to family gatherings disintegrating into emotionally spiked conversations, vibrating with long held resentments, but there was something still and almost teasing in Sandy's voice that made Natalie stop and look closely at her.

Sandy came into the room, placed the bottle on the coffee table, put her hands on her hips and leaned in close to her mother who was lying on the couch. "Don't you think it's time he knew?" Straightening, "I mean he is getting married." And so this is how Johnny found out he was the illegitimate son of the woman he thought was his sister. In the car later when he drove her home, Natalie said, "But really, what does it change?" And in his mind he thought *everything*, but did not answer. After he'd dropped her off, alone in the car driving home, he watched the roads change from major thoroughfares, narrowing into the streets of the neighbourhood where he'd grown up, where his friends lived, where everything that he could remember happened. It felt to him as if a mystery was churning high above him, a revelation that would descend and all the elements of his life would fix into their place. Something on the rim of his mind, his ability to know, teetered there and when he parked and walked past the familiar streets and scenery to his apartment building, he felt radiating out from him not regret, but a loss that he attributed to the imminent loss of this neighbourhood, with its childhood memories, and the quieting sense that this was how it was meant to be.

On his wedding day, the thoughts of his mother and grandmother were put aside and it seemed his happiness could seal off all ambiguities and recriminations, if only temporarily. With a rare effusiveness he joked with his friends, watched the wedding crowd grow on the walkways and steps and called out to people he recognized. That is until he saw his mother, his true mother as he thought of his grandmother, and sister arrive. When his sister saw him she gingerly stepped over the grass in her high heels and when she reached him he left his group and said, "Don't make me tell you again, Mom will be at the front table. She raised me. Remember?" He turned back to his friends and Gus noticing her for the first time said, "Hey Sandy, save me a dance, eh?" But she ignored him.

"What's her problem?"

"She's her problem," Johnny said, jostling Gus, and snorting a laugh when Brad said, "yeah, she's female, isn't she?"

Beside Amy, and like her, Lawrence looked down at the people who milled about in front of him. On the other side of Amy his aunt Dorothy and cousin Claire were fussing over Claire's hat. Lawrence folded his arms, he wore black-framed glasses and an expression that looked more like a sneer than a smile, but was in fact an indication of shyness more than malfeasance. So thin, he looked lost in the loose suit his mother had borrowed from her brother.

"Big day," his uncle Joe said after he moved from the path to stand beside Lawrence, turning to view the crowd. He was a rotund man with a face that turned scarlet at the slightest exertion or risk of embarrassment. Lawrence had lived with him and his aunt Dorothy when he was six years old, after losing his father to tuberculosis, and his mother to a sanitarium for the same illness.

He had originally gone to live with his uncle Norman, who was in his mid-fifties at the time and, with his wife Nora, ill equipped to care for the taciturn boy who rolled his mashed potatoes in bread and hid them under the counter rather than say he could not eat anything more. After this was discovered and weeks went by when Lawrence's shy nature meant he did not speak more than a few words at a time, Norman and Nora became flustered and overwhelmed. When their attitude toward the boy hardened they called Dorothy and said they just couldn't look after him. Dorothy was already caring for Natalie. "Well, what's one more?" she said to her husband in a resolute way, but resolution was not an easy stance for Dorothy and so regret or something closer to anger at her fate took root and she became silent and stern.

Norman and Nora were on the lawn of the church, smiling simply at the line of bridesmaids and the groom with his ushers who were standing in a circle smoking and brushing off the parking lot dust from their clothes. Now in their mid-sixties, the couple wore clothes of a muted colour—on this day, a bulky rose-coloured coat with a lambskin collar for Nora and a grey duffle coat for Norman, heavy winter clothes.

Lawrence remembered how, when he was five, he'd wake in the spare room of their house where he slept those months after his mother was hospitalized: the year 1947, the light through the window falling on an assortment of clothes, furniture, a crucifix over the bed, the sound of traffic from Laurier Avenue, the slow, dreaded walk to the kitchen where food always awaited him. It was then that he learnt the body continues its routine, even if the mind and the confused core of a person becomes static inside. What had they thought at the time? That he could be the son they never had? These people who lived alone, obsessed with their infirmities, Norman's diabetes, Nora's stomach ailments, who had a strict schedule of activities—shopping on Monday night, on Tuesdays listening to the radio while Nora knitted, visits to family members on the weekend. This child, quiet as he was, was such a disruption that they were thrown off balance and their inability to extend themselves to include the boy revealed the narrowness of their lives. And the simple truth, that they were deficient in a certain basic kindness became unavoidable, so that they perceived at the core of their life together an emptiness, the thing that also ironically linked them.

Lawrence watched his aunt and uncle and for the first time felt sorry for them, for their age, for the thickening of their legs, for the difficulty they had walking and hearing. "Yes, it's a good day," he said to his uncle Joe, whom everyone in the family liked, so pliant and kind was his nature.

"Where's Sophia?" Lawrence asked after the silence stretched away from them. Sophia was his Uncle Joe and Aunt Dorothy's only child, a girl of fourteen.

"Over there, standing with Jim and Glen." She was a slight girl, with dark hair, wearing a plaid jumper, smiling quietly at something Glen was saying.

"Oh yeah," Lawrence said, "I see her now." He noticed that since he'd last seen her she'd grown taller and as if to hide this fact, she stooped slightly and seemed to look and listen to her cousins in a shy, off kilter way.

※

Sophia didn't really want to stand with her male cousins. She'd have much preferred to be one of the bridesmaids, wearing a purple, flared dress and wide brimmed hat, standing with them, like one more flower of the bouquet. She hated her dress with the ardour and concentration only a fourteen year old is capable of; she hated its somber colours and Peter Pan collar, this dress her mother had chosen at a store in one of the better shops in Brockville where they lived. When her parents dropped her off at the church and went to Natalie's house to help with the bridal preparations, she joined Jim and Glen and tried to fight the anger that simmered slowly within her. She noticed her mother and father had come back, bringing her cousins Amy and Claire, but she kept her gaze from them, unwilling to be caught in her mother's cloying attention. She saw them by the front steps, her father speaking to Lawrence, her mother fussing over Claire's hat and was glad their attention was diverted. Sophia's grey eyes looked blue in certain light and she was only beginning to display the beauty that would distinguish her in later years, but on this day she thought of herself as awkward, unattractive, certainly not pretty enough to be a bridesmaid. These bitter thoughts occupied her and made it difficult to follow Glen's stories and jokes.

As her cousins spoke, she watched the groom behind them, joking and pushing his friends. She'd met Johnny a few months earlier when Natalie and he drove to Brockville to introduce him to Dorothy and Joe. After a meal of potato salad, grilled vegetables, ham and chicken ("he may not like ham, not everyone does," Dorothy had said when planning the meal), Natalie and he had taken Sophia for a ride in his car. Sophia sat in the back, the same spot where she usually sat in her parents' car. Except before her, on that day, was a version of her future: they listened to Buddy Holly as Johnny drove smoothly over the familiar streets of Brockville. He laughed and said, "We tell Amy that there's a tiny band in the dashboard, that that's where the music comes from." Natalie sang along with the radio, ignoring him, her hand out the window, moving dart-like on the current of air. Watching the groom on his wedding day, Sophia remembered her alert feeling sitting in the back seat of the car, listening to him and Natalie speaking, and feeling a sense of muted dread at the utter familiarity of the streets and landmarks, as they headed back to her home.

"Hi, Sophia," Johnny called from his group when he saw her looking at him.

"Oh, hi." And he turned to his friends as she gathered her attention back on her cousin Glen who was now speaking about his friend's new sports car.

"So, when will Natalie be here?" Lawrence asked his uncle.

"Your Mom said to give them half an hour or so, so I guess it's time to go get them." But Joe did not move, instead he folded his arms across his chest and looked out once again over the crowd before the church.

"Joe," Dorothy called. "Joseph," her strident voice woke him from his contemplation. "Isn't it time to go?"

It was a short drive to the house, three blocks that brought him from the busy street of the church into the heart of the nearby housing development, and as he drove he thought of the wash of change that had led to this moment, and how it felt for this instant like there was a slowing, a pivot, so that he could see from its vantage the past and the future. Was it for this reason that when he parked in front of the duplex and walked slowly to the door, he was reluctant to hurry? Why, when he knew that the crowd he just left by the church was anxious for the bride to arrive, to start the day, did he stop before ringing the bell?

But June answered the door before he rang could ring. "She'll be here in a minute," she said, and Joe could hear the rustle of Natalie's gown, like a premonition, the sound in his imagination of a mythical creature perhaps, from a tale told in his distant childhood.

"They should all be in the church by the time we get back, and the bridal group in the front hall waiting," he said. "Except the photographer, that is."

"Good." Because their conversation was tinged with suppressed excitement, they were looking at each other closely until they realized they were not speaking and a glance so intimate passed between them that they both simultaneously looked away.

"Natalie," June yelled.

"I'm right here, Mom."

"Well, good. Let me carry the train of your gown." And the three of them carefully moved out to the car, depositing Natalie in the back seat, as if she were the wedding cake that her aunt Rita was, at that moment, worrying about.

The ride back to the church took less than four minutes. Natalie looked at the streets of her home; there sat the neighbourhood bully who tormented Amy and Stevie, on the stoop of his house watching her with uncharacteristic awe, and there on the corner, the house of her best friend with someone in the back yard hanging laundry, common, human activity, piqued with a significance Natalie felt but could not name.

By the time they arrived at the church the lawn and pathways were clear. The photographer was standing by his car, struggling with a lens case, but when he heard the gravel from Joe's car, he looked up and smiled. As he did, a long ash fell from his cigarette onto his camera and he stood abruptly sweeping it away, blowing onto the lens. "He smokes too much," June said absently. When the car stopped, and the door opened, Natalie emerged, one delicate foot at a time. She stood finally, clutching her bouquet to her waist. *What is that sound*, she wondered, until she realized it was the sound of her flowers shaking against the satin of her wedding dress.

※

"Beautiful," the photographer said. And Natalie smiled, with her hand on her Uncle Joe's elbow, and her mother crouched, trying to keep pace, holding the train of the gown, she walked the pathway to the large cement steps, where Amy had just been standing, thinking about her bride and groom, thinking how unfair life was and that she'd never forgive her aunt Margaret. The doors were propped open at the top of the stairs. She could see rows of heads in the pews and people standing in the vestibule and could hear a loud clatter of voices until they were overtaken by the sound of the organ, and her pace, and the pace of her heart, fell in line with its rhythm.

STUDEBAKER

The car was a black 1951 Studebaker, with rounded bumpers, running boards along the side and padded benches upholstered in heavy grey corduroy that squeaked when you sat on it. When the snow started my sister, Natalie, her boyfriend, Johnny, and I were on our way home from my grandmother's house where we'd picked up a birthday gift for my brother. The radio, on low, played "Chantilly Lace" by the Big Bopper, and when I asked my sister where the sound came from she explained there was a miniature band, smaller than any of my dolls, locked in the dashboard of Johnny's car. Then Johnny and my sister turned to each other and laughed. "That's right, kiddo," Johnny said without looking at me. I felt small between them, and angry at their teasing, so I tucked my chin into the scarf my mother had tied around my neck and looked at my boots. They were made of brown rubber with metal side buckles, fluffy rims, and came to the edge of the seat, larger by far than my actual feet.

Even though she was only seventeen, to me my sister was grown-up; she was given the task of looking after my brother and me, making our meals and supervising our nightly baths. This was the winter my mother began work at a dinner club called The

Red Door in the west end of the city. The entrance door was indeed red, and shaped like a cartoon version of a door, higher on one side than the other. She began as a hostess and was expected to dress formally. I remember her leaning back to make sure the seams on her nylons were straight and her slip not showing below her dress—a dress that tightened at the waist and flared to just below the knees. She wore lipstick and often her front tooth, which stuck out slightly, would show a small smear of red. The chore of beauty, its routine, the care it demanded in choosing clothes or ensuring that hair curled or hung a specific way, was always a major concern to my mother and sister. In later years it would be my inability to care about such rituals that would define me as a different sort of woman.

My sister was beautiful. She had sandy-coloured hair, green eyes, arched eyebrows, a nose as perfect as a cat's, with full lips and I knew, even as a child, that strangers looked at her differently than anyone else. Beauty tells us there is an ideal, one that the mass of us with normal-sized eyes, a mouth just a little too low on the face, or a nose slightly misshapen or large, never attain. On this night, Natalie was wearing a scarf over her head, tucked into a long bulky coat. When static overtook the song playing on the radio, she turned it off and started humming "You Are My Sunshine." She'd often sing this song when she bathed me, or made toast in the morning, and her humming of it now seemed wrong, out of place, adding to my fear that we would be stuck here, away from home in the cold.

Johnny turned the wipers on and was staring with intent past their swish into the storm. He was a tall, thin, twenty-one-year-old, who already had a job at Canada Banknote where he made printing plates, and he and my sister were talking about getting married. She still attended high school and spent more than an hour each morning, fixing her hair and makeup, singing Buddy Holly songs and jiving with the door jamb in front of the mirror as she tried on different clothes. My favourite of her outfits was a dark green skirt made of felt-like material with a puppy near the hem, and a leash that meandered around the skirt to the waist. Sometimes she wore a crinoline, and its rustle would wake me, when she'd stand on my bed to view herself in the mirror of the vanity across the room.

She unwrapped her scarf and coiled it around my lower face, covering my mouth. As it became colder the wool of the scarf became white from the moisture of my breath, and against my lips felt like gauze. "I don't like the sound of that," she said to Johnny. What she didn't like was the sound of the engine that sputtered, coughed and finally stalled. Heading home on St. Laurent Boulevard close to the junction for Cyrville where the city turned to the country, Johnny veered to the side of the road. "Wait here," he said and jumped out of the car. "Like where does he think I'm going?" my sister said. I had put my head on her lap and she patted my back, still humming. The snow, which had started as tiny picks of ice on the windshield, had thickened and was now obscuring our view of the street. During our drive, there had been other cars, moving as cautiously as us, but gradually fewer and fewer were seen, until it seemed we were alone on the road. When we had sputtered to a stop another vehicle slowly approached and when it drew up beside us, two boys Johnny knew jumped out. They yelled hello to my sister through the window and went to where Johnny was standing. We heard one of them say, "Thought we recognized this old rust bucket," and then they buried their heads under the hood. We heard their voices, punctuated by snorts of laughter, continue in the jovial, jostling way of boys.

It was a school night, which meant my sister had homework and chores to do in the house and after a few minutes of listening to Johnny and his friends, she said in a pointed way, "What's taking so long?" waking me from near-sleep. Johnny came back in the car, "It needs a boost but the guys don't have their cables, so they're going to call a tow truck. They can drive you home, if you want." When he said this, I thought of the rooms of our home, of my mother in the kitchen, my brothers upstairs, and of the dinner smell of potatoes and sausage, still lingering in the air. "No, we'll wait with you," Natalie said. She shivered and moved her hands from my back, and rubbed them together. When I looked up she did not look down and I saw determination in the outline of her jaw.

It turned out to be a long wait as we watched the snow's slow falling, the way it silently and steadily collected on the road and sidewalks. At first my sister and Johnny talked back and forth over my head but soon their conversation slowed and stalled. Our breath created a layer of frost on the windows and Johnny used the scraper to scratch thin ribbons of it from the windshield, they fell on the dashboard like shaved white chocolate. But soon he gave up clearing the window and tucked his chin into the collar of his coat and we continued to wait.

Silent, cold and shivering, I thought of my father, of driving in his 1947 Plymouth, when he was still well enough to drive. In this memory it was a clear winter day. The sun made the buildings look hard, as if they were covered by a lacquer. My father used arm gestures out the window to indicate if he needed to make a turn, and I wondered what they meant and wondered too where in the line of cars at the light we would end up, that it must mean something to be first or third, to be in a black car, to be the fourth child of my mother. And the red and green of the signals, everything was a clue, a matrix of order and meanings. As I grew older, I lost this sense that there was a design to everything, but in those days I saw a deep significance in colours and numbers and those tiny fates, like where you end up in the queue at the traffic lights.

A few weeks after that day, my father became ill and retired to the upstairs bedroom where he was to spend the rest of the winter, his last. At night we'd hear him recite the rosary, and the chant would fill the hours between early evening when we were put to bed and the morning, when my mother would wake me and my brother, when she would make us boiled eggs and finger toasts and I'd watch the yolk spread into the bowl, like a leaky sun.

By the time my father died he had been moved to a hospital, an austere building in the west end of the city. The room where he lay with three other men was overheated; the radiator hummed and a ceiling lamp spread a dirty light over the walls, the beds, and metal furniture. My father sat up to speak, his voice low and his hands shook, and what he said trailed off into silence. In Johnny's car as I lay my head on my sister's knee and she moved her mittened hand to my back. I remembered the last time I saw my father: his new frailness, the faintness of his voice as he tried to speak to my brother and me.

The man who arrived in the tow truck had a cropped white beard and small dark eyes with a woolen toque pulled over his forehead, and when he knocked to tell us he was there his face through the window frightened me and his anxious expression reminded me of a large fish appearing at the glass of an aquarium. Johnny jumped out of his seat, his hands still tucked under his arms, bounding from foot to foot. My sister and I heard the man say, "Lots happening tonight, five boosts in the last hour alone." While he talked and Johnny continuing moving to stay warm, the man put his head under the hood and I heard him clanging tools and attaching cables from his truck to our car. Johnny came back to the front seat, started the engine and it roared to life, with the same force as the relief that flooded me. The man standing in front of the car smiled at the sound.

My sister kept her arms around me to keep me warm and no one spoke on the way home; we watched as the streets became more familiar—there was the home of Alexandra, my sister's best friend, there the house of the retarded boy who swept the street in the summer, and there, finally, was our home, the red brick duplex with a white door. The awning over the front door was under an upstairs bedroom—this was to be my room, years later when I became a teenager, where I would lie and listen to the rain falling on the awning like a scatter of coins. But this was years before such thoughts would claim me, and by the time we got home my brother had been asleep there for hours.

The porch lamp lit the mounds of snow on either side of the walkway with a warm yellow light. We parked on the street and my mother met us at the door. Before she could speak my sister said, "I know, Mom, but it wasn't our fault, the car broke down."

"Oh my God, you could have frozen out there." She took off my mitts and rubbed my hands between hers. "Let me see those paddy-paws." My mother wore an apron over her grey pencil skirt, the skirt she had worn to work, and her hands, when she took mine, felt smooth, like worn velvet.

Sixteen winters later on our way to Santa Cruz in California, I again found myself in a car beside my sister, this time the 1970

Nova that she had received as part of her divorce settlement from Johnny. I was visiting, on holiday from my first job. In the mornings when I woke in the spare room of my sister's apartment, with the sun shining through the blind and the sound of traffic at that coming from the nearby highway, I'd think of the bus I took to work in Ottawa how at that moment it would be stopping to pick up the same passengers, and how if I were there with them we would be pulled through the same routine of streets and traffic.

By the ocean in Santa Cruz it was windy and cold enough to wear a jacket, although the sun lit the buildings on the shore with a blinding light. The restaurant where we ate was empty except for another couple. "It's a work day, that's why it's so quiet," Natalie said. "You should see this place in the summer, it's crazy."

Our table was under a dirty window that looked out at gulls drifting on strong currents of sea air, and after we ordered, we turned from each other to watch the movement of the birds and waves. In this cushion of quiet, with the ocean spread out like a moving sheet of diamonds, Natalie said, without preamble, "I feel at this time in my life a need for happiness". She wore her hair, now blonde and long, in a ponytail so that when strands broke free and fell in her face she'd pull them behind her ears, which were tiny and pale as shells.

"Of course that's true," I said. "But what about Sam?" Sam was Natalie's seven-year-old daughter. "How happy is she?"

"Don't you think I've thought of that?" she turned to look at me, her voice now alert. "You know, you're really becoming judgmental." At that moment the waitress, a young woman dressed in shorts, sandals and a T-shirt, placed our meals on the table—pasta and seafood for me and breaded shrimp for Natalie.

"Sorry, didn't mean to," I said. "But Mom's so upset, that's all."

After lunch we walked on the boardwalk, looking out to the ocean, listening to the music and laughter wafting from the carousal of the amusement park and the sea lions barking from the lattice of beams below us. We talked about our mother who'd begun a new job, working as a sales clerk in the drapery department of a large store downtown and how she was coping with my brother, Stevie, who lived with her after his hospitalization for a mental breakdown. When I finally gathered my courage and broached the subject of Natalie's divorce, she told me that she was just so unhappy with the routine of a housewife, that it seemed as if life was passing her by. Despite the sense of goodwill that had been part of the day, that had made it easy to laugh and talk, there was now irritation in her voice when she spoke of her life with Johnny. She leaned against the rail, turned her face into the wind so that her hair whipped the air like angry ribbons.

Natalie's apartment was accessed through a long veranda lined with baskets of hanging begonias and urns of roses on trestles. It was scented by a perfumed breeze that moved in during late afternoon and walking along the veranda, we could smell roses and feel the cool of the approaching night on our bare arms. As we neared Natalie's door we could hear Johnny speaking loudly to the neighbour who had been minding Samantha. "Good," he said when he saw us, "can you tell this person that as the father I can take my own daughter." I had not seen him since he was home at Christmas five years earlier, when I was still a teenager and I noticed he'd gained weight which gave him a substantial, prosperous air. Dressed in a suit with the tie pulled open, against his tan his teeth gleamed white. When he noticed me, he gave me a slow smile and said in an altered, softened voice, "Well, look, it's kiddo."

"It's okay, she can go with him," Natalie said to the woman in the doorway, while looking between Johnny and me. "Sorry I forgot to tell you he'd be over to pick her up tonight." Samantha came out on the veranda, glancing back at the woman who was gathering her purse and sweater and said, "See I told you," taking her father's hand. She was a clever child who stood alert but quiet as Johnny spoke with me. "Any chance you can come over, maybe have a meal?"

"I don't know when that will be," my sister said before I could speak. "We're supposed to go away to the beach tomorrow and won't be back until a day before she's leaves." Johnny's gaze moved from me to her, but he gave no acknowledgment that she has spoken. "Well, kiddo, give me a call before you leave. If there's any chance, I'd love to see you." He leaned over and kissed my cheek, "Your Mom okay?"

"You know, you don't have to wait until my sister's here," Natalie said as she bent down to kiss her daughter goodbye, "You can ask me about Mom anytime."

After they left, she said, "Why does he do that? Like I'm invisible."

"I don't know, maybe he still cares. You can't blame him for that," I said, as we unpacked the groceries.

Her movements became brisk and she clanged the cutlery as she arranged it on the table. "You're young, you know, you haven't been married, so all I'll say is 'just wait'."

When she put a vase of daisies, cold cuts and salads on the table and then opened a bottle of wine without speaking to me, I said, "I didn't mean that the way it sounded, but it must be hard for him that's all, I mean you left, anyone would have trouble with that."

"But what you don't understand, what is never said, is that I left for a reason." She put the wine bottle down on the table between us.

"It wasn't a whim. I was deeply unhappy." Her feet in their sandals looked compact and perfect, like the feet of angels carved in stone. Her brow was pinched, her stance defiant and beauty, ephemeral as perfume, seemed to radiate from her like heat. When the doorbell rang, she turned from me and said, "That must be Ron".

When she opened the door he said, "For my girls," holding up a bottle of wine. A boyish looking man in his mid-forties, he wore a plaid shirt and jeans with a crease down the center of each leg.

When we were alone in the kitchen after dinner my sister said, "Since he left his wife, he's been living with his parents, and his mother does his ironing." She was leaning against the counter, drinking wine and watching me scrape the plates into the garbage bin. "She'd dress him in a little sailor's outfit if she could." I straightened, laughed and lifted my glass, clinking it against hers, "To your happiness, sister" and her smile faded slightly but she returned the clink.

"Yes, to happiness," she said.

Later in the evening when the conversation turned to Canadian winters, she said to me, "God, remember that night when we were stuck in a snow storm on St. Laurent Boulevard? Remember how cold it was?" Ron had never lived in a place where the snow stayed longer than a day and because whatever Natalie said interested him, he asked questions about the storm. She told him how the tow truck arrived, about the man whose job it was to roam around in the night helping people, and how grateful our mother had been to see us by the end of the evening. While she spoke, I remembered sitting between her and Johnny as it became colder and quieter. "Oh yeah, it was terrible, I thought we were going to die out there in that car," she said.

"I didn't know that," I said and she gave me an annoyed look.

"You were a kid, what, six, what would you know?"

She was leaning across the table, her eyes clear; the glow from the overhead lamp highlighted her cheekbones and soft lashes. "You know what I kept thinking, strangest thing," she said looking at me as if the memory had just struck her, and perhaps it had. "I kept thinking if something happened to you, how angry your Dad would be."

"Really, but he was dead by then."

"I know, weird, eh? I didn't think about myself or even Mom, just him."

Ron was watching her and smiling. "Was she always like this?" he asked me. "Always so concerned about you, her little sister?" Before I could respond he reached across the table, took her hand and kissed the tips of her fingers.

"All I remember is being relieved when the car finally started and we were able to go home," I said. But there was more I remembered: the silence in the car before the man arrived to help us, the cold that made my feet numb and the tight way Natalie held me once the car started to move.

On a cold day in January 2006, I picked up my sister at the airport. Our mother, who'd been living in a seniors' residence and then a nursing home, had taken what the doctors referred to as *a turn for the worse*. When I spoke with Natalie two days earlier, I pictured her on the back deck of her Los Gatos home and imagined the sun and heat caught in the yard, warming the palm trees and flowers and settling on the orange tree by the side of her house. It was the home she shared with her fourth husband who spent most of his time in a room referred to as the games room. I had visited her once at this house. "So what's the problem?" she asked when I called. I told her what the doctor had said, about the marrow of our mother's bones no longer capable of making white blood cells. She asked questions I'd not thought to ask the doctor and then waited for a response, finally agreeing to come as soon as she could arrange a flight. "Do you think Frankie should come with me?" she asked, but before I could answer, she said, "I'll just wait and see."

Two days later at the airport, I stood behind the partition with a group also waiting for passengers. We were dressed in heavy coats, unbuttoned in the heat of the airport, mitts and toques protruding from our pockets like tongues.

"God, it's bitter," my sister said on the way to the car, "How do you stand it?" She had a suitcase that she wheeled behind her and the sound echoed in the covered parking lot. "So, what's the doctor say now?" she asked once we were settled in my car, a rusting 1993 Honda with a faulty heater and radio.

"Nothing much new," I was straining to see if another car was approaching and deliberately avoided looking at her.

"Well, there must be something new."

I saw then my mother as she had been that morning, when her attendant, a large black woman named Evandie, arranged her thin legs so that a pillow separated her knees, and then covered her with a blanket leaving her frail hands over its cuff. Her eyes had a milky appearance and she often slept with her mouth open, the sound of her breathing filling the room. "I've arranged a meeting for us tomorrow with her doctor," I said as I maneuvered the car out of the parking lot.

Natalie's hair was the colour of mink, with honey blonde streaks. She wore a camel hair coat and her suitcase was plaid with colours that matched her coat and trousers. Now in her early sixties, she looked affluent, with a beauty that had settled into grace. In many ways she was never more beautiful, the elegant wave of her hair swept off her neck and held in a French roll behind her head. And even though her face had changed over the years, the skin slackening about her jaw line, there was a serenity to her movements that was indeed beautiful; reminiscent it seemed to me, of a yacht gliding by in sunlight. Her perfume, a light, summery scent at odds with the frigid grey world we drove through, filled the tight space of my car.

The night before there had been a storm and snow lay in the fields on either side of the airport highway, dusting the road with white. As I drove through the desolate stretch leading to the main roadway, my sister said, "I'd forgotten it could feel like this," rubbing her hands together for warmth. As we approached the city, the fields were replaced by apartment buildings and strip malls and I asked her about Samantha. "She's fine, I suppose. She lives in San Francisco with her boyfriend, works for a publishing firm, but she doesn't seem to have much time for her old mother."

"What about Johnny, does she have time for him?"

"Ah, that's right, you always had a soft spot for him, didn't you," she said. "You and Mom," opening her purse and retrieving her sunglasses. "Well I don't know if she does or not, because I never speak with Johnny." We drove in silence for a few minutes until we stopped at a red light. "You haven't asked me about Frankie."

Frankie had been the CEO of a high tech company and had been fortunate—Natalie said intelligent—enough to get out before the bottom fell out the industry. She'd worked for him as an executive assistant when she was married to her third husband, a man I had never met, but who she said drank too much and made passes at all her friends. "It was a bad time in my life," was how she summed up the years—five in total—when she had been with him.

"Why didn't he come?" I asked, referring to Frankie. I had met him a few years before, when I stayed with them. He was gregarious, with a deep tan and a propensity to talk about golf, his own games and other matches he'd seen on the television. He had dark hair rimmed in grey at the temples, his laugh, which was frequent and often unexpected, was a loud bark, and he kept his hand on my sister's elbow when they walked, as if steering her.

"He's never met Mom, so what would be the point?"

It began to snow and I turned on the wipers. "It always was so pretty," Natalie said. "I remember the first snowfall of the year, when I was kid, it was magical." She straightened the purse on her lap and I knew there was something she wanted to say, "Look, I've been thinking, it might be better if I stay at a hotel."

Since my divorce, I'd moved from the small town where I lived with my husband to Ottawa and a second floor apartment of an old Victorian building on a block of duplexes and old townhouses. Even though the street linked to one of the busiest in the city, it was also a place safe enough for cats to roam and where people played tennis in a park that I could see from my living room window. The old oak trees along the street were huge, the span of the branches covering the walkway of three or four townhouses; their gnarled, rough trunks emerged from the earth like powerful torsos. This was the image that came to mind as my sister spoke, those trees standing above the street, their proud and protective stance, as she continued to tell me how much easier it would be for both of us if she stayed at a hotel. She said she knew I'd always disapproved of her choices, that over the years I'd made that obvious. "So I think it would be a good idea to stay somewhere else, it just makes everything easier."

"What are you thinking?" she said when I did not respond, and I realized she was interpreting my silence as contemplation. She turned slightly in her seat to look at me and when I glanced from the road to her face it looked soft, matted, like velvet. I wanted the comfort of her touch, or to lay my head on her lap as I had so often as a young child. I wanted to reach over to touch her face and feel the warmth of her cheek. "What?" she asked and when I didn't answer, "What was that look for?"

"I haven't told you this, haven't told you much about my divorce at all, but he left because he had become unhappy." I slowed and then stopped for a red light. "He said he fell in love, but I knew before that, he was unhappy. It was why he fell in love." I had turned to look at her, at the way she watched me. "And well, I came to understand he had no choice. His leaving was almost organic, it was so intrinsic to who he is."

"I'm sorry Amy, really. Marriages ending, it's always sad."

"Not sure why I'm telling you this, but I was thinking about where I live now, my apartment, how I like it and I guess it's just, well, hurtful to think you won't stay there with me," I said and then looked back to the street which had widened to four lanes as it approached a major intersection. Cars careened around us, held in a tight pattern of movement and time, a complex and reckless order.

"Well, I guess I could stay," Natalie said, searching through her purse for a tissue, which she used to wipe her nose. "It'll be like old times."

"What?" I said. "You can dress me up? While I stand on a chair and complain?" She laughed then, as we merged with the traffic and followed the lane to the Queensway, continuing the journey to our mother's nursing home, and the next few weeks filled with heartache, and finally grief.

US DOGS

In winter the world turns dark early, evening spreads through the yards as the sky turns deep navy, and then us dogs, with the tender light touching our coats, wander through the back shadows, shifting the tall grasses, our paws flattening the fallen leaves. On a day in mid-December I spent the afternoon with the boys and Peggy-Sue, four of us traipsing the trails and sniffing the cold ground, the grass, the tree bark, anything that could tell us what animal had passed by, where there had been a fire, a storm, a death, all the tales that told the past from that patch of land. The snow that year was late coming; the earth was hard though, waiting. The cold, salty smell of winter had settled in the brittle weeds, on the stones and rocks.

Purdy, a matted black Lab, bigger than I was with a soft wide nose, yelped. He was standing in front of a rubber boot in the high weeds beside the swamp.

Yapping, Cracker, a caramel-coloured mutt, part terrier with soft curly fur and a short tail, stretched his neck to sniff. He'd often snort inexplicably and had a nervous jumpiness, so that he would startle when I'd bark at him for entering my yard or chase him from his noisy flirtations.

Peggy-Sue circled from an adjacent clump of bushes where she had just caught a whiff of cat. Her fur was wiry and she had white markings on her face, chest and paws that stood out against the black of her hood and cape.

Purdy sniffed the boot again, as if he recognized it.

Barking, I looked down from the slope of a hill where I was watching them, their heads facing the boot, circling it. This discovery was the sort of thing they'd yap about for hours, after they each took a turn shaking it.

Peggy-Sue loved to hear her own voice barking; she'd bark at the water flowing, at a bird that flew too close, and once I saw her barking at storm clouds as they moved across the sky. When her bark irritated him, Purdy would often growl back, flicking his tail and walking away.

I would have joined them with the boot except at that moment I looked up to the sky and saw the day's light had started to dim. It filled me with the urge to leave, to make my way home to the back porch, through the fields tinged with night, and wait for the boy, for my dinner, for the day to complete its change from day to night. While I sat on the veranda, no animal, dog or human, crossed the alley behind my house without my bark telling them what I thought of their trespassing. My mouth was perfectly suited for this purpose; it was wide, set in a smile, and I could get a good bark behind it. I enjoyed barking; I enjoyed the eddy of sound it made around me, the way it stopped other animals and made them pay attention, show respect.

When I saw Cracker, who I'd left with the boot, trampling the weeds and high grass in that mindless nonchalance I knew so well, I growled at him and he yelped back. With the commotion, the woman from my house came to the door. "Duke," she called, "Come here boy".

I would always go to her, forgetting my anger, because I liked her. I liked that she was usually in the kitchen and there were smells from what she was cooking, so there were always scents and warmth that felt good against my fur and paws. She stood by the door, her hair in a ponytail, wearing slippers, and scolding me as I approached her. But she liked me too; I could tell, she'd rub me behind the ears and when we were alone in the kitchen she'd often take a small piece of meat from the roasting pan to give me.

I liked the children too, three girls and the boy; it was only the father I learned to avoid. When he was home, it was either quiet in the house or there would be loud voices between the father and mother or the father and the two oldest girls. He'd sit in the living room, snapping the pages of the newspaper as he read, complaining and muttering. A smell followed him into the rooms where he sat, a smell like something burnt, smoldering and I knew from the mother's silence and the tension it created that it was best I left. And so often in the early hours of night, I'd meet the dogs in the nearby fields where a sort of camaraderie would touch us, just as the moonlight touched us, so that we'd roam together, listen to the sound of the woods around us: the bird's caw, the rustle of bushes as we trampled, and behind it all, traffic, sirens and voices. These moments with the pack, moments with the cool air in our fur and the feel of stone under the pads of our paws, were the moments that furnished my wandering dreams and made me twitch while I slept in my bed beneath the kitchen table.

Most days when I'd return to the back porch in late afternoon, the boy would be sitting on the stoop wearing sneakers that were grey and brown from dust and mud. He'd ruffle my fur and we'd wrestle in the high grass. Then he'd find the stick and throw it to the end of the yard. I felt the cold air in my lungs fill me with a kind of glee as I chased the stick, grabbed it in my mouth and ran back to him. I could feel my tail swishing behind me and that made me happy too. Then the boy again threw the stick, and again I chased it and when we heard the woman call, we both went in the house for supper, like two brothers.

His sisters preferred the cat, a sleek grey animal who spent her days sleeping and when awake stretched and yawned and tried to ignore the ruckus of the house. I knew she saw me as a nuisance; I was loud, dirty, I brought the smells from the outside into the house and I always panted with excitement to play. She watched me with her yellow eyes, then licked her paw as if finding it delicious, looking down from the sofa, and yet I remember when I first came here to live, feeling lonely from the loss of the warm, squirming spaces of my puppyhood, she had let me lean against her to sleep.

The father was short, the same height as the woman, always dressed in dark, heavy clothes, even in summer, and he was unhappy. I could smell that on him too, just as I heard the constant hum from that seething place, where he lived, alone and hating. I'd seen this condition with dogs too, unhappy and usually sick dogs that you could never approach, who would growl without warning and were never part of the pack. I knew this man had the same kind of feral bitterness at his core, I could feel it when I was in the living room, sitting on the floor beside the woman when she'd lean down periodically to rub my ears. When I looked over at the man I saw that his hostility and anger was the trail he made through life.

Sometimes he'd catch the woman looking at him and growl, "What the hell are you looking at?" and she would look away but I'd keep staring. Yet it wasn't for me that he saved his most hardened contempt. "I said, what the he'll are you looking at?" At such times the woman would try to leave the room without speaking but often he'd jump from his chair and rush at her, at times hit her, so that she squealed and raised her hand to her head. After the fight, when she and I were in the kitchen and she was making him a bologna and mustard sandwich, she cried without making a sound.

Whenever I saw the man on the street, he was closed in, with his head bent down, ignoring the teeming, loud life he was walking through. Even the woman, who'd sit in the kitchen looking through the window that framed the static image of the backyard, sat in a muted, unconnected way. She'd look up stoically, drink a cup of cold tea, glance at the yard, and look down again to her hands. There'd be only her and me in the room, and it would be one of those bleak days when the sky was blank as cement and the weak light showed the yard worn in places to earth, the fence bent to the ground where the kids had trampled it for a shortcut. I'd nuzzle my nose into her limp palm and sometimes she would stop and speak to me, cupping my face and patting the top of my head.

I enjoyed the sounds that lifted from the street, sounds of children chasing each other, televisions heard through the windows, car tires squealing. The street was a stew of such sights and sounds, of smells, and by the time I was four, I knew them by heart, as I knew the members of both my human and dog packs. My life was fashioned from these patterns, times with the other dogs, with the family, times on the streets, in the backyard, sleeping under the kitchen table. How I came to love the smells, a roast cooking in the house, mud from the paths in summer, the scent of burnt leaves, or the cold, wet feel as I rolled in the snow. My life went on in this way, and could seemingly have continued like this forever, except for a day in mid-December of the year I was four.

The marigolds that the woman had planted close to the house in spring had decayed and were mouldy and their bitter scent filled the back yard. When I arrived home, I found the boy waiting on the back step. He picked up the stick and without saying anything threw it to the end of the yard and I dashed after it; there was nothing that could have stopped me, not the cat's disdain, the settled cold of the air, or my own tiredness. We played like this until the woman called from the kitchen, "Don't go away, I may need you."

In the last few months, a stuffy smell had invaded the kitchen, similar to the early spring smell of winter's rot. When we were alone, the woman seldom patted me. I noticed too that she'd stopped humming, that she would often rub her forehead and speak to herself, even as she worked about the kitchen, peeling vegetables, moving from the stove to fridge, her slippers shuffling along the linoleum, a cigarette in the ashtray on the table. The man too was quieter, but this had come as a relief. I seldom saw the girls but lately the boy seemed to have grown wary of his parents, quiet when they were around and even with me a bit slower, less likely to play. On the porch that day after the boy tired of our game, the stick kept taunting me, but rather than react, I lay down beside the boy, resting my head on my paws.

I heard the man arrive home and call out the woman's name and then only minutes later angry voices came from the living room. This was not unusual except on this day she called for the boy and then we heard her say to the man, "Because I have to."

To this the man replied, "You're an idiot if you think I'm going to let you go."

I noticed two bags by the front hall when I came into the house after the boy opened the door. The woman had her coat on and was in the process of tying her galoshes, "I don't want to fight. I just need to leave." She turned to the boy at this point and said, "Please try to understand. I love you, I do. And I'll be back, but right now I have to go." The boy was standing in the doorway between the kitchen and the living room. His parents stared at each other and ignored him. And then the man rushed toward his wife, pushing her against the door as the boy hurried to her side, facing his father, "Let her go. She'll come back; just let her go," he said.

In response to the smell of fear and anger that was everywhere, I barked, barring my teeth, as the boy tried to hold me back. I jumped on the man's thigh and the boy grabbed his father's arm so he could not reach me. We were caught like this for a moment, maybe two, when the woman slowly—as slowly as cats circle each other before pouncing to fight—reached for her bags, her gaze not leaving the man's face. Once she had them, she turned quickly and left the house.

Then she was gone, her absence forcing time to resume. The man kicked a hole in the wall and cursed loudly and the boy hooked his finger on my collar and together we moved through the kitchen to the back porch as the man continued swearing. We sat on the steps as the cold night drew in, both of us trying to ignore the father's rant, which eventually quieted. The sky was huge, full of threatening clouds that gathered at the horizon, and the yards abandoned to the night's descent felt edged in sadness.

Blinking Christmas lights from a house on the adjacent street distracted us as we sat on the porch, the yard in front of us where the season's first thin blanket of snow rested.

After an hour one of the sisters came to the yard to get the boy, who in turn dragged me into the house. I wanted to leave, to find the other dogs and travel to our spot in the field. The sisters made a dinner of macaroni and cheese with wieners, and in silence they spooned its orange curls onto their plates. The boy poured my dry food into the bowl that was kept under the kitchen table and so my munching was the only sound in the room where the boy and his sisters ate. The father ate in the living room in his big chair and somehow his silence over the continuous noise from the TV was louder than any of his rants.

No longer would the woman be in the kitchen if I came home during the day for food or water. And so the boy became the only person who fed me regularly. As he got older and started living beyond his home, becoming part of a gang of boys who lived in the housing project, he'd often forget. And so I'd hunt in the fields and scavenge, checking out the garbage bins at the back of houses and drinking from puddles along the street. At times the neighbours would shout and chase me. But I could always depend on the nearby neighbour, a woman who lived there with her daughter, and who always left bones and scraps on her back porch. The oldest sister left, taking the cat a few months after the mother's departure, and over the next few years the other sisters also went to live with their mother.

When I was in my eleventh year, only the boy, who was fifteen, still lived with his father. The house had become disheveled, and an earthy smell had crept in, so that the inside of the house began to smell more and more like the outside yards. The curtains became frayed, the garden untended and grime outlined the linoleum tiles in the kitchen.

Just as the house had changed, so too in slow stages it had become more difficult for me to walk to the hill close to my home where I'd been going since I was a pup. I had aches, pains; my nails were hard and made a clicking sound on the floor, when I walked around at night, staying indoors as I tended to do more and more. A weariness had settled in my bones leaving me feeling the weight of time on damp days and my coat became matted with burrs, leaves and dried mud. But I still loved the back alleys and even though I'd seen the fields and nearby land be taken over by housing construction, I'd still return to what remained of the field to sit as the sun went down and the air cooled.

Peggy-Sue moved away with her family years ago and Cracker had died, must be a year or so before. Or so we assumed because he stopped coming at night, and the last few months he was there he was dreamy and forgetful or he twitched and barked at imaginary threats. Purdy is much quieter, much slower, as, I suppose, am I.

It is meant to be. I see that now. This quieting of life. I was meant to live my life here, to grieve the passing of those days and nights when the breeze would lift my fur, the sun would warm my paws, nights when the sky turned navy and the moonlight spread into the fields before me like a fog: the path, its weeds and the sullied yards glowing in twilight, its diamond glint as sure, as beautiful, on the trash as on the cars and street lamps. This has been my vantage, my neighbourhood, with its squalor and dramas, its humid nights wired with the threat of violence, its own form of despair. Even my tail feels heavy now and it droops when I walk.

I saw the woman once after she left. She was standing on the street, in front of the house. It was a spring afternoon and she walked by, stopped for a moment and I lifted my head from the cement veranda, sniffed, *could it be, the woman returning?* She was watching each window evenly, when she saw me get up and walk toward her. I could feel my tail swinging behind me. She smiled then and bent to pat my head, "Duke, my God, Duke, how are you boy? Oh, how I missed you." She looked me full in the face and there was something that passed between us, something warm and communal, something that gave me back the memories of those days spent in the kitchen while she baked, hummed, and gave each child a hug when they came home from school. I was young then, spending most of the day curled on a pillow under the table and I'd wag my tail and wait for the scraps, wait for the boy to come home to take me into the yard, and wait for night to come when I could roam the alleyways, and follow the trail to the untamed clearing.

MY BROTHER'S CONDITION

My brother was eighteen when he was sent to the provincial psychiatric hospital. I knew his leaving us was a tragedy because of the way my mother spoke of it, and the sadness that descended on our home. Tragedy suited me then. I could look at it without flinching and say, "So, this is the truth that lurked beneath my childhood." I imagined saying things like that, strong things. I was sixteen and convinced truth was found in tragedy; now, I can't even watch a sad movie.

The episode that led to my brother's first hospitalization, that forced us to realize his behaviour was a condition and not part of what was always considered his willful nature, happened one afternoon when my mother was at work and I was at school. When I came home I found our house ransacked. Cutlery had been thrown on the floor in the kitchen where boxes of cereal and pasta were scattered and splashes of mustard and ketchup streaked the walls. In the living room, ornaments and lamps were toppled; some had been broken and left where they fell.

Three teenage boys my brother had met at a club in Hull who'd come home with him one afternoon were responsible for this destruction. They went through my room emptying drawers of clothes on the floor and stealing my mother's ring and watch. My brother grinned and refused to reply when I asked what had happened. We were arguing when my mother arrived home, when she dropped her grocery bags in the vestibule and sat slowly down in the chair closest to the door, her look one of quiet amazement, as if she was deeply impressed by the transformation of the room. My brother, sitting in the middle of the mess, looking back and forth between the two of us, asked, "What's the big deal?"

"Do you understand, Stevie?" my mother said. "I have to call the police and they'll ask you questions?"

"God," he let his head drop on the back of the chesterfield and stared at the ceiling. "I'll clean it up, for Christ's sake."

"That's not the point."

"I'll get your things back." He lifted his head. "It was just a joke."

My mother was across the room, on the edge of her chair, her elbows on her knees. My brother started to hum, to annoy her or perhaps merely because he wanted to and after a few minutes she said, "I'm taking you to a doctor. This is it. I have to."

"Why? I'm not sick." She left the room and we could hear her in the kitchen, putting pots and pans away and running water to clean the floors and counters. Without speaking or looking at me he got up and left the room and I heard the front door open and close behind him.

※

When he returned three days later, I called my mother at the department store where she worked and she told me to have him stay there until she arrived home. "Yeah, yeah, yeah", he said. He was still dressed in the jeans and denim jacket he was wearing when he left, but they were soiled and dusty as if he'd slept in dirt and his hair hung in his face in dirty black curls. "So, little sister," he said standing at the kitchen table, eating from a bowl of macaroni and cheese he found in the fridge, "How's it been here with Mother Crow?" He smirked, cheese sauce caught in the corners of his mouth.

"Well, she was worried, you know."

"Yeah, I guess," he said, without looking at me.

When my mother arrived home he went to the living room and said, "Look, Mom, I'm sorry."

"It's not that, Stevie," she said slowly. "I have a cab outside. Put your jacket on, we have an appointment." I stood by the front door and watched them leave. My brother turned before he entered the cab, looked back and waved. He looked young and wayward even to me.

※

The first psychiatric ward where he was admitted was in an old hospital in the west end of the city where the grounds were as groomed as those of a university campus. The staff wore casual clothes like the patients and shared an attitude of calm detachment so that often patients and staff were indistinguishable. My brother stayed there for three months, in a private room the size of a cell, which looked out onto a parking lot, a field, and beyond, the highway.

He said that being in therapy was like being in a race or contest. "You sit there and spill your guts and you know how after you puke so much you can't puke anymore? Well, that's how it is there. You keep thinking, well, I told them about my childhood, my father's death, my brother and sisters, and about my mother who no doubt they'll find a way to blame, and they still sit there waiting, expecting."

We were in the sunroom at the end of the hallway. I could see the same flat field visible from Steve's room and beyond, the skyline of the city. It was a bright, cold day in December and I'd come directly from school, carrying my book satchel and wearing a duffel coat, which I kept open. My brother was dressed in jeans and a sweatshirt, smoking a cigarette, his long hair pulled back into a ponytail. His face had an angular look and the muscles were pinched above his eyes as if he was squinting or in pain. It was a new expression, the first sign of the melancholy that would eventually settle there and give him the look of an old man by the time he was in his mid-thirties.

"Do you lie?" I asked. "I mean, it must be tempting, to make up stuff."

"No, the attention is always moving to someone else and some other story." He looked toward the hallway where a man was walking, singing loudly. "There's such sadness in the world, such fucking sadness. I feel it everywhere, as if it's a thick mist I'm walking through." He was growing agitated, so I looked past him to the window where the first signs of night made the sky grow dim. "I've learnt something being here," he continued. "That what we believe is true is really just a product of our mind. Knowing this makes everything less serious." Across the field to the highway, the distant streetlights shone, evenly spaced against a darkened sky.

※

"Stephen is manic-depressive." The doctor was speaking to my mother and me in his cramped office. He was young with long hair that fell into his face as he bent to look at the file. I had seen him on the ward and at first thought he was one of the patients, but here in his office, he spoke with an authority that made his sandals and hair seem like a disguise. "This can be a long term disease, or it may correct itself by the time he's in his mid-twenties. Manic-depression means Stephen's mood swings are extreme and I've started him on some drugs to neutralize their intensity." My mother looked down to the purse on her lap as he spoke, so that he turned to me and said, "Well there isn't much more I can tell you. Everyone with this disease has a different route through it, so I really can't say definitively what to expect".

Stephen left the hospital soon after this conversation. The nights he didn't come home, my mother sat in the armchair facing the door, her legs curled beneath her, the floor lamp illuminating the book she was reading. While I lived out my raucous teenage years, she came to know his illness intimately, its signs and patterns, and she learned to depend on it in a strange way, as you come to depend on weather, mercurial and yet constant.

Within six months, by the summer, it became necessary to hospitalize him again. At times when I'd visit he'd greet me jovially, introducing me to his companions, and at other times he'd be in the sunroom and eye me suspiciously. "Who are you?" he'd ask and when I'd answer he'd say, "Oh sure, that's what you'd like me to believe." And he'd sit and watch the television without speaking until I'd leave.

It was during this stay at the hospital when he didn't improve that it was decided he should be sent to the provincial facility near the St. Lawrence River, a large campus of buildings built more than fifty years before. My mother and I drove him there in a rental car, a two-hour drive through desolate farmland and small towns. I remember the trip, the scruff of fields, the low clouds against a china blue sky, and remember too the weight of my brother's silence as he leaned against the backseat window, a silence broken only by my mother's comments about the distance remaining or the chance of rain.

The campus, composed of twenty or more red brick buildings joined by a labyrinth of pathways and tunnels, looked like a pre-war era housing development. My brother was placed in a ward with thirty other men. During the week when I'd be at school or working in the cinema in the evenings, I'd think of him there in that maze of brick buildings, the alleyways between them and the men standing silently along the hallways. There was something final, extreme, in their condition, as if uncovering truth was the purpose of their illness. I sensed the pursuit in their silence, their disengaged stance and calm dismissal of everything beyond themselves. They shuffled between the dining room and game room to the porch where they would sit or rock and stare at the view from the window. I too came to recognize this view through all the seasons, the lazy flow of the willows' branches on hot summer days, the snow-packed fields of winter, the landscape moving through the months, placid and patient as a parent.

At first my brother seemed happy there. He made friends and played cards during the evenings in the game room. Most of the men were middle-aged or older. Their illness had made them soft, pliant, asking for nothing except the common comfort of the ward with its routine and familiarity. But gradually Stephen became restless, and eventually angry. He told me about games when he threw the cards in the air, "They let me win...Goddammit. They're gutless, taking their pills like scared rabbits."

We heard from the doctor that he'd stopped dressing in the morning and spent the day in his pajamas and robe watching cartoons in the game room, becoming abusive if someone tried to change the channel. One Saturday when I visited, he said, "They're crazy here, you know. Not like the other wards. These guys are the real thing, it's like fucking aliens are running them or something." He looked away, toward the window and squinted. "The other night I woke and Sol, the big one over there, was performing some kind of ritual at the end of my bed." He nodded toward one of the patients, a large, soft-looking man sitting alone at a card table, watching us.

My brother stayed at the hospital almost four years, the years I was in high school. In the end, because treatments of deprivation, shock therapy, and behaviour modification had not changed his condition, because he was not violent and because my mother agreed to care for him, he was allowed to come home. I was eighteen by then, had finished school and I left home shortly after his return. My mother and I argued about the way he moped around the house in his pajamas and ate without speaking. "How would you feel if you went through what he went through?" she said, adding, "The poor kid."

※

After I left home I worked in a government office, and eventually married and left the city to live in a small town. My mother and brother moved into a two-bedroom apartment where he spent whole months in his room staring at the walls, humming songs popular in the sixties, and sometimes disappearing for two or three days, returning tired, hungry and uncommunicative. When he'd leave like this, my mother would call me, upset and worried; she repeated what he'd done the days before he left, what he was wearing, and when he ended up at the hospital she called to ask me to pick him up. When we'd arrive at her apartment, she was at the door, "Oh my God, let me get a look at you," she said and patted his arm or cheek. "What happened? Oh Stevie, let's get you washed up and put to bed." Then she turned to me and asked what the doctor said, or how he'd been on the way home. "What are we going to do?" she asked, frowning and holding the top of her robe or sweater tight to her throat.

※

More than twenty-five years after my brother left the hospital, after he'd moved into a residence for the mentally ill, I found him on a curb of a busy four-lane boulevard, his head drooped, his thinning hair, now mostly grey, long and uncombed. At four-thirty that afternoon, I'd received a call from my mother who waited hours for him to arrive at her apartment and so I came to the city following the route from his residence to her apartment to see if I could find him.

Although it was February and cold, he was not wearing a coat. After I parked the car and approached him, I said, "Stevie, it's me. Amy. Come with me." He wore a shoe on his left foot, a sneaker with velcro fasteners, because his hand shook and for the past few years he'd been unable to tie his laces. The sock of his right foot was wet and had a hole in it. He was mumbling, rocking back and forth. I knelt to speak to him and he managed to raise his head but his eyes could not focus. Cars rushed by on the nearby boulevard.

"That's it, that's it, I know it, that's it," he said over and over, captive to the chant of his own voice. There was desperation in the words, in the breathless way he said them and in the unfocused gaze over my shoulder. He stared ahead, but put his hands on my arm. They were shaking and I wondered how much of it was due to the cold. His cardigan was soiled, and buttoned unevenly; under it he wore a T-shirt that had a drawing of a skull and the words The Grateful Dead on it. Bringing him to my car was a slow process, as if I was teaching him to walk, but when he was in the passenger seat he put his head back and stopped chanting. I thought of the many different types of loss, as my brother and I sat side-by-side facing the front window of my car as if we were moving toward an ordinary destination.

I'd seen him the week before when I visited and he'd been quiet, answering questions with either "yes" or "no," eventually leaving the living room to read in his old bedroom. When my mother and I were alone she said, "He's not doing well, the medication is wrong, I just know it and I told his doctor, but they don't listen." She was setting the table and moving between the kitchen and dining room, bringing in a salad, buns, plates with our dinner of pork chops and mashed potatoes. "You mark my words, he's going to crash. Something bad is going to happen." She stopped fussing over the table and looked at me, the skin between her eyes pinched with worry and her expression created a surge of anger in me, intense and irrational, so that I said sharply, "Mom, I mean really, what can be done?"

I took him to the emergency ward of the hospital where he'd been admitted many times before. There I spoke with the nurses, explaining that over the years he had been diagnosed with a number of mental illnesses, including bipolar and schizophrenia. They took his blood pressure as he stared at the ceiling and then the nurse told us to sit in the waiting area, a crowded room with chairs linked by metal bars. We found two seats together and I picked up a magazine as he tilted his head to watch a TV that hung from the ceiling. He was no longer shaking. The nurse had given him slippers to wear and a blanket to put around his shoulders. The expression on his face, which had alternated from rage to fear to confusion, had softened and for a while we were content, sitting side-by-side, brother and sister, waiting.

I thought of the times, over many years now, filled with such hospital visits, of other times when I'd waited with him outside doctors' offices or emergency wards, and I thought about when we were children, Christmas mornings, and spring days when he'd shout with excitement and drive his bicycle recklessly. I remembered crouching together at the top of the stairs when we were supposed to be asleep, trying to see the television we were not allowed to watch. We'd muffle our laughter and take turns peeking into the living room, until our older sister or brother would catch us and yell, "Get to bed, you kids".

When the doctor examined him he was admitted to the psychiatric ward. We sat together until a nurse arrived to take him there in a wheelchair and when I watched him leave, he looked like any one of the lost and unloved souls often seen in downtown cores, shuffling along in their private world of destitution. He no longer looked like my brother; he'd grown old, his expression dulled and he had a stiff, awkward way of holding himself.

After midnight when I reached the parking lot, the storm that had begun earlier had blanketed my car in a thick layer of snow. Through the front window I could not see other vehicles in the parking lot or the red neon sign that read "Emergency" over the hospital entrance. I knew I'd soon need to drive home, but I was mesmerized by the quiet and I thought of the long process that had led to this moment; how my brother, also by now alone in his room on the ward, was just as solitary. "I wish this were not real," I said aloud, as the falling snow continued to isolate me in my car.

The next day when I visited I was surprised to find Stephen sitting in his bed watching the news on the television. He was dressed and looked clean and alert. There had been an earthquake in Mexico the night before and when I entered his room he said calmly, "Looks like a bad quake."

"Yeah, I heard," I replied. The newscast showed scenes of destruction, store windows cracked, houses reduced to rubble. The announcer spoke to homeowners who had lost their houses and the final image was of a doll wrecked and battered beside the debris of a destroyed duplex.

"Remember that time we ripped the house apart?" he said after a few minutes. "It was these guys I met. I knew they thought I was stupid. They made faces behind my back." I was staring at him and he was staring at the television. "It was wrong what they were doing and I knew it, but I couldn't stop them. That bothered me, that I couldn't stop them." He sounded as if he were recalling a dream, something nonsensical and perplexing. "But I just couldn't. I was paralyzed." He turned to look at me and I saw the pale green of his eyes. "And I kept saying to myself, over and over, but this is real, this is real, this is real."

THE VIEW FROM THE LANE

I leaned against the wall of the laneway beside the house where I grew up. Over the years the neighbourhood—a housing development of red brick townhouses and duplexes built in the early 1950s—had sunk into disrepair and gave off a general sense of neglect and decay. On this day a soft rain was falling and the colours of the pavement, the cars along the road, the wild assortment of discarded toys, bikes, lawn chairs, intensified and became shiny as if the objects beneath were melting. I was eighteen and this was to be the last season I lived here.

Vancie, the boy who lived in the adjacent duplex, walked into the lane, saw me, put his head down and moved out to the street, his hands stuffed in his pockets, shoulders hunched against the wet cold. He ignored me even though we'd known each other for years, had attended the same school, suffered the same winter afternoons of drowsy heat that oozed from radiators, and walked the same streets home at the end of the day. I'd seen the quiet resignation of his mother, as she hung laundry or sat on the back porch drinking coffee, watching the afternoon creep into evening.

She wore faded cotton dresses over her thin form, with an apron that was always weighed down from clothes pegs in her pocket. And I remember her in a snowstorm, on the evening of her husband's death, moving slowly along the path leading to her home. These are the kinds of memories a neighbourhood like this can hold, the silent fall of snow on an evening full of loss, the muddy streets as spring nudges us into another year, or the hardening of colours on an autumn day.

From the lane I saw the spot where at five I'd played marbles with other children who lived on the street. Boys on their bicycles circled, cracking the layers of ice that floated, brittle as glass, on puddles. I'd left the house without boots for the first time that year, loosened my jacket and breathed in the raw smell of earth. I crouched on my knees clicking the marbles scattered on the hard ground into a hole the shape of a fist. I liked the sound of their click and the hard feel of them in my hand. Later I emptied my winnings on the chenille bedspread in the room I shared with my mother now that my father was dead, so that they pooled together, tiny planets, in the middle of the sagging mattress.

Before my mother went to work and I started kindergarten, when he and his brother were in school, we often visited Vancie's mother. We'd sit in the living room, the women drinking coffee, talking and smoking while I sat on the floor in front of the television, watching soap operas where women in chiffon lived out their inexplicable lives. These characters never had conversations like my mother and Vancie's mother had—complaints about the cost of food, their careless children or loud neighbours. Later though, after my mother began to work in a department store, she stopped seeing Vancie's mother except when they'd pass in the laneway or on the front path and my mother would say, "Oh, Louise, how are you?" and Louise would answer calmly, but I could tell there was a disappointment between them, a distance that kept their conversations short.

Early summer days the year I was eight, when sun lit houses, awnings and porches and I was on the street with Vancie and other neighbourhood children, we'd swing on railings, play hide and seek, run from porch to porch, gather on front lawns, scatter to back yards and collect again into groups in laneways, creating a strata of noise largely ignored by the adults. I hid beneath rusted cars, behind the garbage shed in my own back yard or under a nearby veranda, playing until my hands became stiff from cold, until the sky darkened, and my mother came to the back porch, calling my name.

Sundays I attended mass, moved from sunlight into the dark vestry, smelled wood polish and smoke from the censer, knelt and followed the priest in prayers. Tablets marking the stations of the cross lined the nave; the solemn statues of saints and martyrs, their placid hands raised in the sign of the cross, stood in contrast with the crowded, noisy streets of that neighbourhood, just beyond the church's huge silence.

I'd often see Vancie chasing his brother on the pathway behind our duplex, pathways I also followed coming home from school, trampling the trail between the yards where the dogs roamed, long grass scratching my legs, a smell of rot and decay being released into the bright air. A clean sharpness marked the end of summer and the lawn mowers, bicycles propped up against the brick walls, the cars rusting in laneways, so familiar I no longer saw them, suited the autumn coolness and added to the disorder. These yards were full of wild tufts of abandoned grass and earth pounded to a claylike hardness. It comes back to me, this time, with all the permanence and insular quality of an island seen from shore, a compact time, the lull between childhood and adulthood. It was full of earnest, humourless effort and the ordered sense of my place within the single files of the schoolyard, in the pew at church, and within the rooms of my house.

The nuns who taught us guarded the schoolyard like black crows, their faces stern, as they gathered us into rows in hallways or stood before us in the classroom. I dressed in the black watch uniform my mother had ironed, with knee socks that gradually slouched to my ankle forcing me to bend every five minutes to pull them back up my leg. I'd sit before my mother as she braided my hair, feeling the tug of her impatience. After school I practised baton routines and in the autumn marched in a parade, dressed in a majorette outfit with tassels on my boots and matching sequined hat. The studious, careful handwriting in my new scribblers indicated the seriousness of my intent during those years, an approach that was to fall away as I became older, when the patterns no longer held the same sense of purpose.

At fourteen when I woke in my dimly lit room on a winter day, hearing the television below me and my mother in the kitchen, I moved to the window to see the sky's anemic blue. I had begun to feel that life was elsewhere, past the yards, the glum rows of houses, past the field of snow between the school and industrial park, past the railway tracks, creeks and fields that marked the boundary of my neighbourhood. Out there, somewhere. I did not want to turn back to my room, to see the bed, the desk against the wall, chipped and shabby, to feel the inherent aimlessness in these objects. But I did turn from the window, left the room, moved through the house, onto the street, and although I'd done this many times, I did it now with a sense of detachment, as if I were somewhere high above my own lone figure walking along the street, looking down at the miniature houses, the yards in stamp-sized squares, at the tree branches like exposed nerves, and at myself, the single figure focused on escaping those streets, fighting through the acres of heavy space, hunched against that winter day. Suppertimes, when my family sat around the dinner table, their faces over the plates were as blank as fingernails and their conversations equally bland.

Walking to high school I had to cross a major thoroughfare into a more affluent neighbourhood of bungalows and two-storey houses. I grew to know the moods of those streets, to know how evening fell by four o'clock as winter approached and the houses isolated by the cold of those winter mornings. I knew the trees along the road that in autumn shed their leaves and in winter stood like etchings against a white linen sky. My days then were divided into classes linked by crowded hallways, and my mind was consumed by now forgotten, but at the time, crucial intrigues. For years I trudged this same route, past the long line of houses, recognized as markers to my way home. I traveled the route so often that it seemed my life would always be the same, but years later when I found myself unexpectedly back there I remembered the way the streets looked through the seasons and remembered too that sense that nothing would change, and yet everything had.

When I was sixteen I used to see Vancie's girlfriend standing in the laneway between our two houses while he worked on his car. I knew her because we were in the same class at school. She'd see me too, and sometimes look away, or sometimes greet me. "Hi, Amy. What's new?" This was the summer a boy was murdered not far from our home, one hot night in July. Both Vancie and I were in the crowd that had gathered, both of us had seen the boy stagger and fall, coil around his death like a shell hardening. Standing in the eerie silent heat, I looked up to see Vancie across from me, staring at the body of the dead boy, until one of his friends hit his arm and said, "Let's get the fuck out of here." I too left quickly, returning to the steps at my back porch where I could feel the splintered wood of the veranda under my bare feet. The air was swampy and I was fanning myself, drinking a soda when I heard the sirens and saw Vancie approach from the unlit path at the back of my house. My mother came to the back door. "Is that Vancie?" she said. "What is he doing out there in the dark?"

A day in November, a few months after the murder, when the first snowstorm of the year began and large flakes fell, slowing time itself, the houses of the neighbourhood hunkered down against the new cold and snow covered the flowers already dead from an early frost. It was still snowing at four o'clock in the morning when the sound of a taxi woke me. At the window, I saw Vancie's mother hesitate in the back seat, then move onto the path where Vancie met her, putting his arms around her shoulder, and together they began moving back to the house. The next morning at school I heard that Vancie's father had died of a heart attack at work the day before.

By the time I was eighteen I lived alone with my mother. My sister and oldest brother had married and my other brother had been hospitalized for manic depression. In my room under the window where the bed was, on late spring mornings before leaving for school, I would wake to see the curtains move from a weak morning breeze and to hear the swarm of children's voices below on the street. The sound flooded through me and I longed to return to sleep. My mother downstairs made coffee to take to the back porch, where she sat on a lawn chair and listened to the children. I'd imagine her there, staring ahead, thinking of my brother in the hospital, at intervals the cup in her hand rising to her mouth. I knew if I were downstairs, the sight of her would make me want to escape the house, the neighbourhood and the day, so I stayed in bed as long as possible.

Alone that afternoon in the living room, I turned the television off and sat in a hot silence with the curtains backlit by a bright sun that would have flooded the room if open. Panic and an inability to move overtook me, as if I were being held underwater. The room with its mismatched furniture: chairs, a large chesterfield, tables, the television with rabbit ears perched unevenly, a grey area rug and beneath, worn wood floors, all lay in silence, as if the space was holding its breath. *There is no escape*, I thought, closing my eyes against the room and the moment.

)(

Years later, when I'd moved back to the city and was on the bus waiting at a traffic light of an intersection close to the neighbourhood where I had grown up, I saw a man leaving a three-storey apartment building and thought, *could that possibly be Vancie?* It was a late spring day, the snow was melting and what remained was sooty and partially dissolved, so that it looked as if banks of black lace rimmed the walkway. I could see water in long braids of light and shadow moving along the road into the gutter. Houses cowered beneath the simmering clouds of the approaching storm. It was a day not unlike the day I stood in the lane watching the street when Vancie had passed me without speaking. An ordinary day, when nothing exceptional happened. The man was smoking and he frowned as he looked away from the traffic. There was something in the slouch of his walk reminiscent of Vancie, reminiscent of that street with its sense of ruin and neglect. I could not tell if he was content or saddened by where his life had led him, and I thought, as I waited, that maybe it's not that simple, that maybe I'm not meant to know. When the light turned green, the bus drew up beside the man and I saw him flick his cigarette butt into the ditch, saw him turn to look toward the traffic, and saw behind him a heavy sky with grey clouds pressing down hard on the scene.

SUICIDE NOTES

When I think of Landy, as I often do, I see her sitting in the kitchen of the house where I lived as a teenager—the table shoved under the window, thick bands of sunlight streaming in from the backyards divided by an assortment of bent and uneven fences. She lived at the end of my street, beside a neglected field, and in grade nine we'd meet on the path behind the church to walk to school. Our long hair straight—mine dark, Landy's sandy blonde—we dressed in short skirts and leotards, our eyes lined in black. The year was 1967. We viewed the ruckus around us—the loud gang of teenagers, streets with cars lining the curbs and the mess of bikes, lawnmowers and abandoned vehicles in laneways—with melodramatic disdain. This brooding landscape crept into us, of this I am sure, and that at the core of our lives—we thought in such broad terms then—there was a kind of shapeless despair.

One humid day in the summer I was sixteen, walking to the corner store, wearing flip-flops, cut-off shorts and sleeveless T-shirts, our hair in ponytails, we passed neighbours who also suffered the heat, some drinking beer on verandas, others lying half-clothed on latticed lawn chairs. "Well, there's a pretty sight," Landy said, moving her head in the direction of a neighbour. A large woman dressed in a bathing suit that seemed to expand with soft rolls of skin like rising dough, she was moving the hose over her legs and feet, sitting on the distressed rim of her child's plastic wading pool.

"Cute," I said, wiping sweat from my upper lip.

"Are you going with Jimmy to the drive-in tonight?" she said. Most Saturday nights that summer were spent there, in Jimmy's car, or in the unpaved parking lot by the concession stand, where a crowd of us stood as the night came in and cooled our bare arms. The music from car radios and the smell of popcorn and marijuana surrounded us and became the air we breathed. Behind our talk and laughter, the intrigues we created, movies played on, their images of high-heeled women and adventurous men in air-conditioned rooms contrasting to the close summer heat, the unceremonious slurp of soda and the outline of our feet propped on the dashboard.

"Yeah," I said, "Where else would I go?"

That night, alone in the back seat of Jimmy's car, her legs stretched out, crossed at the ankles, Landy said, "I hate this movie. It's so lame." She wore blue jeans, ragged at the knees and hem. "Don't you think?" Her blue eyes huge, larger even than was attractive, gave her a look of someone frightened or overly alert. Her lips were full and her nose had a stubborn groove at the tip, something she hated. Both her parents were Italian, "red-blooded," she said. And she was thick boned, not dainty as she wished.

From the front seat I turned to look at her. As a staple of late night drive-in movies, we'd seen the movie, *The Birds,* many times before. "Well the part with that guy in his pajamas and his eyes pecked out," I said. "That's pretty scary."

"It's a dummy, you know, dressed up; it's not a real person," Landy said.

"Speaking of dummies dressed up, look who's here." In the line of parked cars in front of us a group of teenagers surrounded a blue and white 1957 Chevy. Some of them were leaning in the windows or against the doors, some standing outside in groups of two or three, smoking and laughing, and as we watched, a boy and girl moved behind the car directly in front of us. He had grabbed her hand and she was trying to yank it back. The boy, Maurice, lived one block over and the year before had been Landy's boyfriend. "What a dickhead," she said.

Jimmy came back from the concession stand with a bag of popcorn for me and strawberry liquorice for Landy. "Hey, I saw Robbie in there. He's here with Maurice, said we should go see them."

"Yeah, we know, there's Chevalier right there," Landy said. She'd given him the name Chevalier after they broke up. "Who does he think he is?" she said, "Maurice fucking Chevalier?"

"And, look, he brought his car," Jimmy said. "He loves that damn car."

The girl Maurice had been pursuing finally broke free and ran away as he yelled after her, "You're not worth the chase."

Landy said, "Yeah, Chevalier's Chevy, I remember. Let's go over."

"Why?" I said.

"Let's just go," she glared at me. "Why do you have to always question when it's something I want to do?"

Later with Landy and me in the back seat of the Chevy, Jimmy in the front, the movie scene we'd discussed began, when the mother walked past the chipped teacups to the hallway and the bedroom where she'd discover the corpse. Maurice was outside leaning into the car at the driver's window. "That's so stupid," he said. We turned to the screen. "Like that could happen."

"What do you think, Maurice?" Landy said. "That movies are supposed to be things that always happen? Like maybe they'll put a camera in your living room and put that on the screen? Yeah, that'll pack 'em in."

"Why are you such a bitch sometimes?" He stood and walked over to a group of friends at the back of the car.

"Thank God, he's gone," she said. "One more minute looking at that face and I was going to shove something into it."

We turned to watch the movie, the mother now racing away in her truck, then pushing the lovers apart as she ran into the house. "Oh no," Landy said. "The damn armrest just fell off."

"What? Are you kidding?" I said. "You know he's going to kill us, right?"

In Jimmy's car ten minutes later, we crept away from the field of docile cars lounging in front of the screen, where now a flock of birds were swooping down on a group of schoolchildren, "You did it on purpose, didn't you? Landy?" I said.

"Well, it was loose, that's what gave me the idea."

The car crept to the exit, its lights off, when we heard Maurice. "My armrest. Who broke my fucking armrest? Everyone. Out of the car. Now." His voice grew distant, lost to the crunch of gravel under the wheels and Procol Harum's "Whiter Shade of Pale" low on the radio. It was then, when we reached the gate and the road leading to the drive-in, that we broke down laughing, *laugh attacks* we called them, when we were unable to stop the flood of laughter erupting from somewhere deep within us where everything seemed irrevocably funny.

Shortly after I met Landy, her mother was admitted to the hospital with what was then referred to as a nervous breakdown. At the time she was convinced that members of her family had been taken over by other people or forces not to be trusted. When I went with Landy to visit, we found her mother in the sunroom, staring out the window and refusing to look at her daughter. "Mom," Landy said. "I'm here with my friend, Amy. Remember Amy?" She looked up at us, suspicious. Her eyes, pink-rimmed, gave her a raw look as if even the sight of us caused her pain. "A friend," she said slowly.

The day she came home from the hospital a month later, she planted herself in a large, ripped chair, her hands clutching its arms, her gaze never leaving the television. Eventually, though, her suspicion abated and she again began to take part in her routine: working as a secretary at an insurance company, cooking supper at night, singing in the kitchen on Saturday mornings. A large woman, Landy's mother had a beautiful face, framed by thick black hair cut short, and her eyes seemed the colour of some changeable gem. I'd hear the swish of her nyloned thighs and always knew where she was in the house, so heavy was her step. But her voice was light, pitched with a high lilt, as if she was trying to catch her breath. I can see her still, sitting in that ripped lazy-boy, rubbing a foot, "My dogs are barking today," she said. And the incongruity between her words and the sweetness of her voice gives a comic overtone to the image.

)(

Landy was the middle child, between an older sister and younger brother. Her sister, Honey—I never knew if this was her given name or a nickname that stuck—was known for her drama. It was in her attitude and appearance; her features pronounced, heavy arched eyebrows over nearly black eyes, and her lips red and thick. It was beauty skewed somehow, beauty recognized because of its uniqueness. Her thick hair was so black it shone blue and flowed down her back to her waist, mane-like, or she'd pull it from side to side as she spoke. Her friends were always about the house, laughing as they moved en masse to her room upstairs, or standing in the vestibule, animated and high. Often I smelt marijuana when I came over, but Landy's parents seemed to not notice. "Honey tells them it's incense and they believe her," she said, her voice tinged with contempt. Honey was two years ahead at school, but when I'd see her there she'd pretend she didn't see me. "She's just a bitch," Landy explained when I asked why.

)(

"My paws are frozen," I said one winter day on the way to school and Landy responded, "Fore or hind?" We were walking hurriedly, not bothering to do up our jackets, even though it was twenty below, occasionally chanting under our breath, "fuckin' cold, fuckin' cold, fuckin' cold".

A clump of kids walked ahead of us, lured to the school as if we were all under the same spell. "Idiots," she said with her head bent.

"What?"

"Those kids, look at them, brainless monkeys, and look at those two." Those two were a couple walking on the outskirts of the rowdy group, the girl pulling her coat closed and carrying a purse that looked like my mother's, with a tiny, stiff clasp on the top, while the boy hovered over her in a protective way, an arm along her waist at the back. Landy said, "Looks like that stupid arm of his is glued there." Unlike the kids they were with, the couple looked straight ahead, not speaking or laughing. "Leave them alone," I said. "They're in love."

"Yeah, right." But I knew she didn't want to talk about them and we continued walking in silence. I knew too that an unrest was brewing in her. Usually her anger walking to school was preceded by an altercation—as she called it—and usually this altercation was with her father. He'd come home drunk, argumentative and there'd be shouting and cursing, sometimes hitting, and then the police would be called. Once she'd shown me bruises and when I said it was not right, that she should tell someone, she replied, "Don't worry, now he'll feel guilty and give me money."

He worked sorting mail and wore the navy blue uniform of the Post Office with his name, *Ray,* stitched in gold on the breast pocket. I have memories of him in the doorway of their kitchen, dancing and singing show tunes, his favourite "Oklahoma," his high voice in contrast with his stocky build, the disheveled sandy blond hair and bushy eyebrows. He filled their home with a sense of dangerous gaiety as he made potato chips from scratch, dressed in pajamas, his slippers shuffling across the linoleum, and he renamed me Audrey because he said my name did not suit. "What were your parents thinking?" he asked.

I'd been fatherless since the age of four and it fascinated me how Landy loved and hated him, how there was this center in her life that wasn't in mine. It made me see the way I lived alone with my mother—now that my siblings, a sister and two brothers, were gone—as somehow lopsided.

After school our habit was to come to my place; my mother worked and was not home until after five o'clock and even when she was there, in contrast to Landy's home, mine had an atmosphere of consistent calm. We made toast, sometimes with honey or jam, and sat by the kitchen window when she'd say, "Okay, so what would you write?" And we'd start composing the notes we'd leave to be found after our suicide.

"I mean think of it," she said as I sat over the notepad, pen poised, unable to think what to write. "Nothing you would ever write could ever be as interesting as your suicide note."

"Yeah, so what would yours say?" I said.

"I kind of like the simple, classic message, something like, *fuck off, just fuck off all of you,* maybe or, *I'm doing this so that I'll never have to look at your face again.* Then the person finding it would wonder if it was meant for them."

"I'd want to settle scores," I said. "And then be gone without hearing the response."

"You see that's your problem. You'd start writing and then that way you have of trying to see all sides of something, you'd still be writing the next day, and when would you actually kill yourself?" The bread popped. I went to the counter, smothered the toast in butter and brought the plate back to the table. We were drinking tea. I tried to think what I'd write, gazing out the window at the sullied yards, but my attention was drawn again and again to the sound of the television on in the living room.

"How about this: *This morning I saw the enormous schnoz of Mr. Halpenny and thought I could no longer live in a world with such ugliness.*"

Landy said. "It was kind of the thought I had when I saw him, only it seemed it should be him who should die, not me."

"There's lots of examples of ugliness at school," I said. "There's that smell that radiates off Mrs. Chadwick."

"Yeah, her whole body smells like feet. And then there's that near-sighted idiot Mr. Moran." Whenever Landy spoke with him, she'd call him Mr. Moran, and he would patiently say, *No, Mr. Moran, with an 'a'*. And she would then say, "Oh sorry", but continue calling him Moran. "He thinks I'm slow, that I can't remember," she said.

"This would be funny: *I can't stand for one more minute to live with the memories of what Mr. Grant has done to me, horrible things, involving dogs and leashes, and so this is my only recourse.*"

"That would be funny and mean," I said. Mr. Grant was a shy, withdrawn Geography teacher, who had trouble meeting your eye when he spoke.

"Well most funny things are," she said absently, intent on her writing. "*I bequeath my family to science. Studying them should explain why I am doing this.* What do you think of that one?"

"I think I'd stick with the one you wrote the other day, what was it? Oh yes, *what excuse can I make except I'm inconsolably bored.* I like the 'inconsolably', I like that word," I said.

"Or something concise, obvious: *I'm sick of this waste of time.* Or: *What lies ahead doesn't look good, so I'm checking out now.*"

We heard the sound of quivering violin coming from the soap opera on the television. "I know," Landy said. She was animated and looked pretty, her eyes wide and full of good humour. "*I leave you the deceit, the cruelty, the stupidity. Have fun with that.*"

Later, on the chesterfield, watching the gauzy scene of a couple embracing, she said, "See the way the camera stays on his face?"

The scene was ending and the camera pulling away from the actor and actress. "That's because he's making her so sick, she's throwing up on his shoulder."

※

Landy's brother Willie was a large boy, with a wide, toothy grin and the same sturdy bone structure as his mother. He was destined to always look like a large boy, even when he was a man. It took me a while to realize what made him different was not that he was simple or slow, labels others put on him, but how fundamentally kind his nature was. His endearing way allowed him a sense of wonder in things others often overlooked. I remember him in the back yard finding beetles and running to show them to us as we sat on the veranda drinking soda and complaining about the neighbours. "Look at this quickly," he'd say. "I have to get him back; I think he's scared to be out of the grass." He rode his bicycle everywhere and enjoyed it in a way we had long forgotten, if in fact we had ever been capable of feeling that kind of joy at something so simple. When the debates and arguments escalated in his home, he would watch the television, shifting position to see his program while ignoring the noise and chaos surrounding him. Landy was closer to him than anyone else in her home.

※

On one of my visits to Landy's house, her father said to me, "Is that your mother who waits for the bus by the rock near Isidore?" He was dressed in boxer shorts, T-shirt, a short robe hanging open over his rotund form, his hair uncombed, and he held a spatula that dripped bacon grease, lifting it for emphasis as he spoke.

"Maybe."

"The one with the raccoon fur coat, the pretty one?"

"Yeah, I guess." I said. The coat was given to my mother by her sister Margaret and when my mother first modeled it for me, I said, "No matter how good it looks, it would always look better on the animal".

"She's a good-looking woman," he said. My mother as pretty was a foreign concept, she seemed simply too functional and accessible to be really attractive.

"Dad," Landy said. "Stop it."

"I only asked Audrey because you wouldn't tell me," he said turning to glare at her.

Landy shoved me into her room. Our homes were part of a housing development and so both had the same layout, but in Landy's house they used the dining room for her bedroom. She had put a blanket up to separate it from the living room, a blanket she pulled back with a clothes peg to open, like a tent. "God, I hate when he starts that," she said.

"Starts what?" I said.

"You know, talking about women." She sat on the unmade bed. The room was dark; the cold of an overcast February day seeping in. "Now that he knows who your mom is, he'll stop to talk to her." I couldn't imagine why he'd want to do this, why he'd look at another woman, when his wife seemed to me quite beautiful, and he seemed instead ordinary, peasant solid, and a bit slow formulating thoughts.

"You see," Landy said. "You see, why I'd rather go to your place?" She was angry with me. She was often angry with me. If

I said something she thought wrong, or even something she did not know and she inferred mockery at her ignorance, she would turn with anger and contempt. "And what do you mean by that? Huh? What makes you an expert?" Her anger often escalated, especially when I refused to argue with her, with her leaving wherever we were—the cafeteria at school, the kitchen table at my place, or walking faster to leave me alone on the road. She'd often turn back to say something like, "Once, just once, I'd like you to say what you really think. But no, you're too spineless."

)(

The pathway beside Landy's house where the dogs roamed was dense with undergrowth, burrs, weeds and shrubs, lined by an old chain-link fence that separated her yard from the school field. A trail, where the earth was worn smooth as leather and children had bent the wire fence, created a shortcut. I have a photograph of Landy on this pathway, her cat, Tigger, on her shoulder. We both had cats, cats that lounged on our bedspreads, jumped on the tables and windowsills, and slept beside us; this love of cats was something that linked us. One of Landy's, a lanky tomcat, had learnt how to open the kitchen door of my house. We'd hear the latch flick and then Junior, as he was known, would saunter into the living room. I heard my mother once tell a friend, 'if you hear the back door opening, don't worry, it's the neighbour's cat coming for a visit,' and it seemed these visits were just one more sign of the eccentric but accepted character of our neighbourhood.

My mother had always loved animals, was always leaving food on the back porch for the neighbourhood dogs and as a result of the affection she held for Junior, Landy and she became friends of sorts. When she'd arrive home from work, stomping snow off her galoshes in the vestibule, Landy would meet her and tell her about Junior's exploits: a midnight stroll into a neighbour's basement, the time he fell asleep in the truck of the man who delivered vegetables and ended up at his farm overnight, or how she saw Junior on the roof of a neighbour's house looking down at the street. And my mother, to my great annoyance, would laugh and say, "That Junior, what a hoot!" My mother's language was a source of constant irritation for me, the most despicable of boys who hung about the streets were *lads,* when something perturbed her she'd say with indignation *oh, fiddledy,* and instead of butt or ass, she'd refer to a person's rear as a *seaty-go-hind.* The way I dressed, jeans with a ragged hem, sweaters too big, my thick black eyeliner and bangs that almost covered my eyes, all these hallmarks of my appearance, she claimed gave her a headache. "Oh, I can't look at you," she'd say, "or that headache will come back." My exasperation was sincere, but to Landy my conversations with my mother were often a source of mirth, something to joke about, or mimic when we were in a crowd.

Near Christmas of the year I was in grade ten, my mother found a batch of our suicide notes and confronted me. "What are these? What are you two doing after school?" I explained they were a joke, that most of them were Landy's, but she stood rigid in the doorway to my room, radiating anger, or perhaps, I realize now, something more like worry or concern. "Can you please tell me how suicide notes could possibly be funny?" she said, crushing the paper in her hand. "No, this is important, you must be careful." And as she turned to leave, she said in a softened voice, "I don't understand you, I just don't understand how you think sometimes." I was glad my mother had not found the last few notes Landy had written, serious notes that she'd not shared or discussed, and that I found only after she left. *There is no end to the pain*, she wrote and on another sheet, *this must end*. The next day when I asked her about them she said she had not meant them, "and besides they're unfinished".

An hour after my mother had asked me about the notes, when I was lying on my bed reading, she came to the door again. "I think I've found a part-time job you'd like." Her friend was a manager at the cinema that was part of the new shopping center not far from our home and she'd told my mother they were looking for a person to work at the candy bar. And so a week later I started work there, making vats of popcorn, selling cola and chocolate bars until I moved to the more lauded position of selling tickets for the movies. It meant that I was not home most evenings, but when I would arrive Landy would often be sitting with my mother either in the kitchen having tea at the same table where we used to sit after school, or in the living room, watching television, Junior curled on my mother's lap.

When my brother moved back home from the psychiatric hospital where he'd been during my high school years, I moved away and began working in a government office, living alone in an apartment in the south end of the city. During the last year I lived with my mother, Landy quit school and worked at a nearby laundromat. The experience taught her she needed her high school credentials and so she began to attend an academy that would give her an equivalency diploma. The program provided a stipend for housing and food, and she moved into a boarding house in the Glebe, where she had a room large enough for a bed, a bookcase and dresser. She shared a washroom with two other people and this sharing provided a long litany of complaints, which I would hear if I called or went to see her. The occupants of the boarding house were mostly students, bleary eyed, coming and going on bikes at all times of the day or night, as well as older destitute people, who lived alone and tried to ignore the students as they raced by. Although Landy was young and a student, she seemed more like one of the older, sadder tenants. The winter I was twenty-one, I used to visit her in the boarding house, when she'd tell me she was surviving on cottage cheese and canned carrots. "It's really quite tasty," she said. "And nutritious." She lost weight and her hair, which she'd cut short, darkened.

Near the end of that year I met the man I later married. He lived in the same apartment building where I lived and had a taciturn nature, which was often mistaken for one of contemplation and thoughtfulness. I would come to think of this year, 1975, as the year my world imploded and the movement toward novelty and increased mobility, which had begun when I was a teenager, started to slow and then retract. When I introduced Landy to my future husband, once we were alone, he said, "Well, that was gross." He meant the crowded room where she lived, the smell of meat cooking in the hallways, the mass of bikes piled near the door like the remnants from an accident. I did not respond and he said, "And she seems weird too."

The following summer I married this man; the small ceremony took place in a B&B in the quiet town where my husband and

I moved after the wedding. Landy came alone to the ceremony and sat with a group of my husband's friends but did not speak with them. Later, I was told they'd laughed at her attitude and appearance, saying she looked like a schoolmarm. When I heard their comments, I felt a pang of anger and a desire to defend her against their jovial, nonchalantly cruel assessment. How could they not see who Landy was, her capabilities, her humour, her uniqueness? "That dress was mine," I said to my husband. "I gave it to her years ago, and besides she doesn't want those goons you call friends bothering her." In the photograph I framed and kept on the buffet in the living room, she stands a little apart from the group, her smile crooked and uncertain.

Shortly after I married I became pregnant and my life became preoccupied with caring for my son. My friendships now were mostly with other young mothers who had children of the same age and my days had become a routine crowded with domestic concerns and obligations. When I'd visit the city to see my mother, I'd call Landy but our connection was growing more and more tenuous.

"What's the deal with you?" she asked one day in a restaurant where we had met for coffee and when the conversation had stalled. "Just happy to be looking after the kiddy?" I could have defended myself, but I saw how her face had aged, the lines pronounced and something haunted in her eyes, which now instead of blue looked grey. Her hair, already showing grey, was pulled behind her ears in a flat ponytail.

"Is that so wrong?"

She looked away from me and I could tell she did not want to argue. "No, I guess not," she said with genuine weariness.

Two years after this meeting Landy moved to Toronto. *An adventure*, she wrote in her first letter after moving, but gradually the letters slowed, and the tone changed. *There's some strange stuff that happens in a big city,* she wrote. She lived a spartan life with a cat in a bachelor apartment off St. Clair Avenue. The walls were soiled looking in the stringent light of that April day when I visited for the first time. In the living room she had placed a single straight-back chair and the large lazy-boy, still ripped, that her mother had sat in for weeks after she was discharged from the hospital. When she made tea and we sat together (I was on the lazy-boy, she on the straight chair), I could hear the sound of water dripping from a roof as the snow melted, and see the view outside her window of old apartment buildings and squat strip malls desolate in the overcast. "So," I said after a few moments of mounting silence, "how are your parents? And Honey and Willie?"

"I don't speak to anyone but Willie and he's okay." Which were more words strung together than she had spoken since I arrived. But speaking of her brother had always lifted her mood and she told me he visited the month before and they'd gone to the nature museum.

"He'd like that," I said. A streetcar rumbled by.

"He had such a bad crush on you," she said.

"Really, you never told me that."

"Oh, yeah, when you married, it broke his heart." She looked down at her hands in her lap and watching her I was brought back to earlier that day when my husband had asked why I was visiting Landy. He was sitting at the kitchen table, reading the paper, and when I turned to answer the early morning light was so brilliant it obstructed my view, so that I could not tell if he was looking at me, or still reading the paper.

"I'm sorry if Willie was hurt. He is such a good person," I said.

"Really?" she said, looking up at me I noticed the slackness of the skin around her eyes. "You're sorry?" She took the shawl from the arm of the chair and placed it around her shoulders. "He'd have liked to know that."

※

More than a year later I received a telephone call from Honey telling me that Willie had died. "Landy refused to call you," Honey said. "But I thought you should know." He was twenty-five and had been hit by a truck while riding his bike on a highway.

The next day my husband and I drove to town and when I entered the funeral parlour the first person I saw was Landy. She was standing near the door, speaking to her mother's sister, a small, darkly-clad woman who wore a tight black kerchief on her head. When she saw me Landy said, "You didn't have to come you know."

"But I wanted to," I said.

The wood-paneled room was crowded with relatives and the sound of their muted conversations; an anxious solemnity pervaded. I could tell Landy had been crying and I noticed her hands shaking.

She took my hand, not speaking, keeping her head lowered, until Honey called her to a group crowded around the closed casket and she left me with my husband, who had just entered the room after parking the car and having a cigarette. He said, "Do we have to stay much longer?" Later, in the chapel, before the service started, Landy came and sat beside me in the wooden pew, leaving her family in the front row. My reluctant husband was on one side of me, Landy on the other, and the three of us sat without touching or speaking for the half hour it took to complete the service.

Almost a decade after Willie's death, on a cold winter day, my husband told me that he'd fallen in love with someone at work and was leaving. My son had already chosen the university he'd attend and I was working in a bookstore on the main street of our small town. I'd be lying if I said I'd not noticed our lives dulling to work days spent apart, nights before a television and weekends when we seldom spoke and we each pursued separate interests. By this time Landy and I saw less of each other and so it wasn't until I'd left the small town that had been my home for almost twenty years and found an apartment and job in the city that I told her of my marriage breakdown. She told me we were destroying more than we knew and on that point she was right. I had no idea how deep the roots had become, how devastating the break. "What did you think, Amy?" she said to me that night. "That you'd call me and I would commiserate and you could feel better?"

 I had moved to an apartment on the second floor of a converted Victorian house, close to the downtown core, and after I hung up, I looked around my kitchen, at the counters stacked with boxes, some still packed, some open where I could see cutlery, plates and glasses wrapped in paper towel. It was hot, a humid August night, and the rooms were small and unfurnished, their walls dull from the overhead lamp that seemed to smear a layer of grime over everything. My two cats milled about, jumped on the window ledge to catch the warm breeze that moved into the room. I sat on the floor and looked at the space about me—boxes and dining room chairs along the wall, curtains pulled back—and felt the muggy air that the ceiling fan drilled down into the room. I fell asleep that night on the floor in the heat with the sound of the fan and the noise from the street outside the window. When I woke the next morning, stiff and late for work, I did not think about Landy and our conversation the evening before, nor did I know that I was never to speak with her again.

⋇

I think of Landy's last day, a few months after our conversation, how the sun rose, and the moments, one after the next, moved along the route of their solid predictability. She would have grown to hate that predictability, the even sure way each anguished moment followed upon the previous moment. She used pills, I never knew what type. I was at work and Paul, a colleague and friend, was in my office discussing a conference we were planning together. He was a precise man and carried a clipboard where he kept notes and information and he had a way of sitting, with one leg folded over the other, that made him look closed in and compact, like a cat. The phone rang and he said, "Go ahead, get it. I'll come back." Honey was on the line and without preamble said, "Landy killed herself last night." I'm not sure what I said, I'm not sure how I was able to write down details of the internment, but when I got off the phone, there they were on the paper beneath my hand.

I remembered Landy telling me about a reoccurring nightmare, *spider dreams* she called them, when a wad of spiders would crawl over each other, a mass of jointed legs moving in slow motion. And sitting there in my workplace, a place where I was someone she would not have recognized, I remembered the dream, the way she'd say in her matter-of-fact way, "Well, I had another spider dream last night". And I wondered then why this memory, from the myriad memories I had of her, arose at that moment.

※

Three years before Landy's death, my mother had moved to a two-bedroom apartment not far from where I worked, and the night after the suicide, when I pressed the intercom to tell her I was there, she made her usual mistake of immediately hitting the entry button.

"Did I do it again?" she said in the hallway when I reached her floor.

"Yes, Mom, but it's okay."

"No it isn't. What if I let in a murderer?"

"I need to tell you something." But I could see she was fidgety, not listening, and knew she thought that her continued confusion regarding the buttons was a sign of advancing mental decline.

"I always think it's the right one and then I question myself and end up making the same mistake."

"Mom, don't worry about it."

We were now in her apartment. She stopped, looked at me. "Is something wrong?"

"Landy killed herself last night." The same sentence Honey had said to me, the same blunt fact.

"Oh." She backed up to sit on a flowered chintz chair, a chair that matched her chesterfield and drapes. "Oh, my."

"It's awful. I can't seem to get my mind around it."

I could hear a loud mechanical rumble, like a garbage truck revving, but it was too late in the day for that.

"Amelia," she said. "You listen to me. She's at peace. This is what she wanted, what she wanted for years. You never understood that about her."

"What?"

"Well, it's true. She was always so disturbed, I remember, everything disturbed her." She sat upright as if what she had to say demanded fortitude. "It worried me, the way you cared for her, the way you'd do whatever she wanted." My mother's cat, a black, sleek animal, jumped on the arm of the chair and she patted him for a moment. "I do feel sorry for her mother though. She was such a sweet woman, way too sweet for that husband of hers." Then she turned to me as if putting the matter to rest and asked if I was staying for dinner. "I made a pot roast and there's too much for one person."

That year, the year of Landy's death, an infestation of black crows hit the city; thousands en masse would land in trees or on electrical wires, where they sat like music notes on a staff, their communal flight creating a sound like huge sheets flapping, their caw filling the air with a dark laughter. The day of Landy's funeral, as we walked to her grandmother's gravestone where her ashes would be buried, crows gathered on the high branches of the trees above us. "They give me the creeps," Honey said. She was there with her husband and two children but her mother and father did not come. Her mother refused to believe Landy was dead. "Mom called her phone and heard the message on the answering machine and is convinced we're playing a hoax on her." I didn't ask why her father was not there. At Willie's funeral he'd appeared deflated and broken and when I tried to speak with him, he was unable to make eye contact. At the graveside were old friends, Jimmy and his wife, friends of Honey, people I had not seen in more than a decade. We formed a semi-circle, Honey beside me and when I joined her I asked the question I had been wondering about since I heard of Landy's death: "Did she leave a suicide note?"

Honey did not look at me but put her arms around her youngest child, a six-year-old girl who wore a puffy jacket of such brilliant colours that it stood out among the mass of dark-clad mourners. "No, no, nothing. They found nothing."

The minister arrived and as he spoke about God and Landy's place with him, words she would have despised, I looked to the sky and remembered when we were teenagers we'd often used this cemetery as a shortcut to a nearby neighbourhood. Its hills were marked with rows of tombstones, and on summer days, were shaded by huge trees that hovered gigantic over the graves.

I remembered then how things we did or stories we told each other could bring on attacks of laughter so violent we couldn't catch our breath, when everything would seem hilarious and absurd. Standing there in the new chill that promised winter, a story came back to me from the year we were sixteen.

There was a tall, skinny boy in the grade ahead of us, whom Landy had nicknamed Vulch, a shortened version of Vulture, because of his stooped stance. His hair was long, hung in his face, and he seemed to radiate the same kind of contempt for his surroundings as Landy. During the year we were in grade ten, she developed a crush on him, "God, he's so cute," she'd say when she saw him on the path before us during our walk to school.

The story I remembered took place on a day when I'd walked home alone and as it was almost spring, I was wearing shoes rather than boots; they were high heels which made it difficult to walk, and almost impossible to walk quickly. At some point in my journey I turned and saw Vulch behind me, his strides long and commanding. I felt imprisoned by my shoes, as if by concrete, they anchored my feet to the ground. And then by what seemed at the time as the cruelest of possibilities and because I was desperately trying to outwalk him—but was in fact hobbling along the street with an awkward and graceless gait—the heels of my shoes, pretty stilettos which cost me a week's salary, became stuck in the grid of a sewer cover, stopping my hurried progress abruptly. I had a choice: step out of my shoes and try to pull them from the grate as he walked by or stand still and smile. I did the latter, and when he passed he smiled too and asked if I was okay. I said, "Yes, just fine."

Later that afternoon as Landy and I walked in the cemetery, it was this event I was recalling. "Oh my God," she said. "Are you kidding? You were standing with your shoes stuck in a sewer? Just standing there like an idiot?"

"I know, I know. But what could I do, get on my knees and try to pull them out of the grate? That would look even worse."

Once her astonishment abated, after she garnered every absurd detail, she began to laugh. "Oh yeah, that's real funny," I said. But then I too started to laugh, which made Landy clutch her stomach and laugh harder, and we laughed so hard and for so long that we had to bend over to stop the pain in our side and catch our breath, leaning against the tombstones, the muscles in our faces paining from all our laughter.

THE MURDER ON
PRINCE ALBERT STREET

He was his mother's first child, born on a cold day in October 1957, when she was twenty. Outside the hospital window the sky was marble hard and blue as the Wedgwood vase her mother had kept on their buffet, a gift, highly praised, from a distant aunt, the same vase that her sister had taken after the sudden death of their mother a year before. She saw this sky change over the day, from pale blue, through stages of royal and navy, to settle, by the time of her child's birth, into a dimensionless black.

The baby's father, a boy of twenty-two, visited her at the hospital the next day. He lived with his parents and had not seen her for months, since she had told him she was pregnant. Her movements were still heavy and her body seemed mysteriously bloated beneath the pink nightgown. The baby was gawky, with short crooked legs that moved aimlessly under the blanket, like a bug caught on its back. "Here, hold him," she offered, stretching the baby toward his father. He held the child awkwardly, looking down at the sore red face.

"What's his name?"

"Joseph, it's a strong name, don't you think?" The father shrugged and handed the baby back to her.

He did not know what he felt, but he knew it wasn't love. There was nothing that made him want to see her or the baby again, and so in his customary way, he reasoned that this girl and her squirming child, with their sleepy faces, were in no way connected to him. It made leaving easier when the next week he packed his bags and took a bus to Edmonton, $300 from his parents in his wallet, and plans to begin a job in an oil field advertised in the Ottawa paper.

The mother moved to an apartment on Somerset Street close to shops and restaurants that catered to a variety of immigrant populations and lived on financial aid through a welfare program for mothers with no other means of support. It was a small apartment, with yellow walls in the kitchen, an old round-cornered refrigerator with a metal handle that took a knack to open, and a stove with burnt on grime around the elements. She didn't miss the boy who was the father even though he was the only lover she'd ever known, even though before Joseph's birth she had fantasized that he would ask to live with her and they would settle into the patterns she imagined made up a family. When she'd sit before the television in the evenings, her baby in his crib in her cramped bedroom, she thought about this boy, the one summer they knew each other, the night at the drive-in when she became pregnant. She concluded it was for the best he was not there, that she could not have felt her contentment had he stayed.

When Joseph was five, he and his mother moved to a crowded neighbourhood in the east end of the city, on the second floor of an apartment building, part of a series of stuccoed buildings with green wooden railings and verandas. Their floors were linoleum and the rooms dark and small. When he started school, his mother began work as a waitress in a busy diner where she met the man whom she would marry, and with whom she would have another child, all within a year. He was quiet and thoughtful and liked to read in the living room at night and because he was fond of Joseph, he adopted him, so that from that time on, Joseph had his last name. Lisa, the daughter, a pretty blonde baby, was born when Joseph was in grade one. He used to sit with her in the kitchen before school and when she'd throw her food on the floor he'd laugh and throw it back until his mother would become angry and snap, "Joseph, stop that, you're just encouraging her". His mother stopped working to stay home with the baby and his stepfather found a job driving a truck that took him away from the family for weeks at a time. Then when the baby was two and Joseph eight, his stepfather had an accident on a winter day on the Trans-Canada Highway and was killed. Because he was hauling dangerous chemicals, the highway was closed for a day and a story about the closure appeared in the Calgary newspaper on January 19, 1965. His mother kept a copy in the top drawer of her dresser where Joseph found it when he searched her room, as he often did in the years that followed, looking for money or valuables. After the death of her husband the mother was forced to move her family to subsidized housing on the outskirts of the city—long streets of duplexes and townhouses, divided by laneways, back pathways, where the sky was cut by electrical wires and the air was full of the sound of children and angry adults. This was where the murder happened, eight years later.

Two years after Amy moved away from the neighbourhood where she grew up, a sixteen-year-old boy murdered his twelve-year-old sister in a house two blocks from where Amy had lived. Perhaps because the brother had schizophrenia, the same illness Amy's own brother had been diagnosed with years earlier, or because she could see the scene of the murder, the dim hallway and small bedroom, Amy became obsessed with the story during the autumn of the year she was twenty-one. She first read about it in the newspaper, where a photograph showed a stretcher taking the body out the back door, the brick walls and wooden windowsills, originally painted white were now yellow and cracked, a bag of pegs sagged beside the clothesline and below was a cement veranda with black metal railings. She knew that beyond what was shown in the photograph was a back yard with rusty bikes and toys, discarded implements, such as hoses, tools, and a lawn worn to earth from the constant running between yards by the neighbourhood children. These were the kind of children you could catch, line up, and photograph, and through the grime of their faces something earnest and alive would shine, so that the photo would be praised as showing the blind optimism of being young. This was the kind of child Amy had been years before when she lived there, running from yard to yard, chasing friends, playing games, panting in the cold autumn air. And this was the sort of child the murdered sister had been. The newspaper showed her school photograph, her unruly hair springing from barrettes and her smile still the innocent smile of a child. She was part of the constant noise that raged through the neighbourhood, like a loose wind, running in packs of children, playing hide-and-seek or chase.

After the murder, the brother stayed in the room beside his dead sister until the next morning when their mother found them. She called the police, and when they arrived, she stood in the doorway as they crowded around her son, asking questions he did not answer. He was found unfit to stand trial and was taken to a psychiatric hospital in another city.

Amy was living alone when the murder happened, working in a government office, and seeing the man she would later marry. Her mother had moved to an apartment with her brother and when Amy told her about the murder she said she wasn't surprised. "There were some loonies there," she said, as if they were cartoon characters. Amy's mother had always been able to disregard incidents she found unpleasant or mysterious, but Amy could not stop thinking about the murder. In her imagining, it was always the deepest part of night, when rows of evenly spaced townhouses and duplexes were caught in a soft darkness that moved like mist among the buildings, thinning under the street lights and thickening in laneways. Sleep invaded every shape. In the October dark, bare branches scratched the sky and the cars along the road, garbage bins on the roadway, the fences enclosing yards, everything still, as if frozen in contemplation.

Time was the real enemy. If it had refused to move forward in that plodding, measured way it had always moved forward, the sister would not have been found. The tumble of rushed images that jammed the room would not have happened—starting with the mother, her shock, then grief and later still, something smaller, poisonous, lodged at her core, the nest of pain and anger that bloomed at times into a profound bewilderment and was to stay with her all the years that followed.

Then the police crowded the room, questioning the boy and taking him away; they took photographs, lingered about smoking, looking out the window, "awful," they said to each other and meant it. The ambulance attendants who took her body from the room came next, each thinking of their own fragmented lives of adulterous intrigues and rebellious children. And a few days later, sent from the city's social services, two women scrubbed the bloodstains from the floor and removed the mattress and pillow.

King George, Queen Mary and Prince Albert Streets stretched in three long parallel rows that spanned the area from Rideau River in the west to St. Laurent Blvd in the east. The streets were made up of duplexes or row houses and were built as affordable housing in the early 1950s. They were red brick buildings with roofs of assorted colours, which over the years dulled to the same nondescript shade of rust. The houses all had the same layout: from the veranda, there was a vestibule, which in Amy's home was always cluttered with shoes, boots and coats, an L-shaped living room, dining room and beyond a kitchen. At the top of the stairs, off the hallway, were a washroom and three bedrooms. Every house started out with the same possibilities. Amy lived there from the time she was two until she quit school and moved away at eighteen. She knew the winter nights when snow glowed in soft mounds illuminated by the street lamp, summer afternoons when the heat pressed upon the streets and stilled time and spring days when the soiled banks of snow collapsed into grime.

After the murder, Amy would wake in the middle of the night and watch the shadows on the ceilings of her apartment crawl forward as the first strands of daylight stretched into her room. Later on the bus, where she found herself part of a herd of commuters being pushed from stop to stop, she imagined the dead sister, lying curled around the sounds of her last day, her friend's laugh, the roar of traffic from nearby streets, the screen door slapping shut when she arrived home and her mother's greeting. The moment when the brother stood outside her door, his hand on the knob, while she was coiled around her dreams, that moment before everything changed, when the tragedy was still a churning thought in his mind. This was where Amy's thoughts stalled as she went through the routine of her day, making coffee in the office, speaking on the phone or typing. She'd glance out the window at the parking lot, where beyond a field lay in the slow process of hardening for the approaching winter.

After Amy married and moved to a small town miles away, she thought less and less of her childhood and had forgotten about those few months when her thoughts had been consumed by the death of a young girl. That was until one Saturday when her husband brought the newspaper into the kitchen where she was pouring a cup of tea and said, "Didn't you tell me about this case?" There, on the cover page of a section entitled *Observations* appeared the same school photograph of the dead girl. The piece was part of a lengthy series about the devastation of mental illness.

She took the paper and her tea into the living room and read the article, discovering details about the murder she'd not known, such as the fact that he'd heard voices and had killed his sister because he loved her and had wanted to protect her. When Amy was finished she put the paper down, looked out toward the street, at the large oak and maple trees that had started to turn colour, and it struck her that the murder had happened on just such a day. She thought about the morning after the sister's death, when the light would have filled the room, just as light was filling her living room more than a decade later. Joseph would have been able to see his sister, her disheveled hair, the sad twist of her ankle exposing the soft pink palm of her foot, so clearly it was as if he were looking through still water. Through the night he would have watched the changing light reveal her body, entrapping her in a stillness before regret, before even sadness.

 As Amy sat in her living room, her legs tucked under her, the tea now cold on the table beside her, she could hear her son upstairs start the shower. He and her husband had planned a weekend away, to attend a hockey tournament and so after dinner there were hours of noisy activity as they packed and prepared for the trip. After they left Amy sat at the dining room table, in the quiet left in their wake. It was unusual to not have the sound of her home interrupting her thoughts, to have the room lie utterly still around her. She looked toward the corner of the dining room, to a dark space beside the buffet, a spot where, at that time of night, light could not reach and she saw there a shifting of dark against dark, a coiled animal of deepening shadows.

Joseph's mother turned fifty-five on a hot summer day. Her job at the time was in a bakery on a major thoroughfare close to the city limits. She worked with the owner, a man of eastern European descent, who had difficulty speaking English, and his wife, a plump woman who harboured a deep mistrust of everyone except her husband. Joseph's mother had worked in this bakery for more than ten years, and while others before her had said they grew infuriated by the impersonal way they were treated there, it was exactly that quality she liked best about the job. Her employers did not know her past, no one in her life at the time did, except Joseph, who had been released from the hospital five years earlier and was living in a group home uptown. He had grown heavy and was barely recognizable as the thin, tortured boy from that summer of 1973.

On the evening of the mother's birthday, she returned to her rented apartment not far from the bakery and watched television. Later she washed her face and brushed her teeth, but when she shut the light and got into bed she could not sleep. She knew that to turn fifty-five alone was a form of failure, but she was unaccustomed to wondering about life, to contemplating what its patterns and vagaries meant, and after many years of cultivating silence her mind had a sluggish quality so that it was only a pained quiet she experienced lying there, staring into the dark.

The next day at work Joseph called, wanting money, and she told him to go to her apartment after she finished work. She hung up the phone, wiped her flour-dusted hands on her apron, when the name *Lisa*, a name she had not thought of for years rang in her mind, like a clear bell. It took her breath away so that she turned from the wife of the owner who asked in a harsh tone, "Was that a personal call?"

When Joseph arrived that night she made him a dinner of macaroni and cheese and gave him forty dollars in an envelope. The television was on as they ate, but over the evening news, she said, "I turned fifty-five yesterday."

"Oh yeah," he said without looking away from the television.

"And today for the first time in a long time I thought about Lisa."

The name had not been spoken between them for years. He was quiet, watching the television, but he knew she was watching him, waiting, so that he turned and said, "I still miss her". How surprising, those four short words, how they were able to deflect her anger so that she saw in them the last, final link between her and her son.

When he was leaving he noticed that day's newspaper and his mother's mail on the table by the door. On the front page of the paper was an article of a teenage boy who had murdered his family in Toronto. He stared at the photo, the boy no older than seventeen, smiling awkwardly out from his school photograph. "I hate reading the paper," he said. After he left she bolted the door, prepared for bed and that night slept soundly in the unforgiving dark of her small bedroom.

ON THE BUS

After Amy finished high school she moved from the home she shared with her mother and brother to a small apartment a short bus ride away. That same month she began work for a government department on the outskirts of Ottawa's east end, and in autumn, as the hours of daylight shortened, it would be dark when she caught the bus in the morning and dark again when she came home in the evening. The fields surrounding the road, bare except for the occasional factory and electrical pylons stretching evenly into the distance, would lie dormant in the day's first or last touch of murky light.

For three years Amy followed this same route, often with the same people, as the bus, on its way to the outlying industrial plants and warehouses, wound its way along boulevards lined by high-rise apartments, strip malls and low-rise medical buildings. When she was older and had lived away from the city for many years, she thought of this time in her life with fondness. She remembered how the bus rides parenthesized her workday and allowed moments of contemplation the rest of the day did not, and she felt protective toward the young woman she was then, captive on the bus beneath a hardening sky and captive to that moment in her youth with its uncertainty, naivety, and promise.

During those years Amy developed a fear that nothing would ever change, that her life would stay forever the closed world of the office, her apartment, the bus and streets she'd view on the way to work, but she was mistaken. One afternoon, at the same instant that the sun poured in the large window of the filing room where she worked, a pipe broke in her apartment. When she returned home that night she was forced to move seven floors up to an empty unit. Seeing the items the superintendent had brought from her apartment—food on the kitchen counter and clothes and toiletries in the bathroom—Amy experienced the surreal sense of finding the familiar in a strange place, as if she'd entered a dream and was captive to a moment when anything could happen.

Her mattress lay on the living room floor against the wall, dragged there by the same man who had brought the food and then shortly after her television. For most of the evening she sat on the mattress and read, disturbed only by the noise from the street below or people coming or going in the hallway. Later in the evening after she prepared to sleep, she turned on the television to watch the news, sitting crossed-legged with her back against the wall. The announcer reminded her of Mona, a woman in her office, who could often be found speaking and laughing with Mr. Raymond, Amy's boss, a man of such earnest attitude and speech as to be a figure of ridicule in the office. His face was sharp featured. "Like a fox," Amy said, to which Cathy, her coworker replied, "or rodent." When he was beyond earshot they mocked his shiny hair and pointed face. "From here," Cathy leaned across the table where they were sorting the morning mail, "he looks like his head is made of patent leather."

"Well, that's perfect, because his face looks like a foot," Amy said.

"What are you two laughing about?" Mona asked as she entered their office.

"Life," Amy said and continued sorting the mail.

)✕(

In the new apartment Amy fell asleep watching the tiny lights from the houses twinkle below and extinguish in a random sequence, until the darkness became a black slate pressed against the balcony door and window. She dreamt Mr. Raymond arrived, dressed in a camel hair coat and pinstripe suit, an outfit she'd seen him wear in the office. He began to undress, fumbling with the buttons of his vest and shirt, undoing and stepping out of his trousers and underwear. After he removed his socks and was naked, he stood straight and looked at her. There was an offering, a vulnerability in his stance, and when he came onto the mattress Amy discovered Mona lying beside her. Her eyes were closed, and although during the day she never wore makeup, her mouth now was red with lipstick and she was saying his first name over and over, as she put her arms around his neck and drew him to her. Slowly he moved his hand over Amy's arm and smiled while Mona whispered. Amy jerked awake remembering in that instant that she'd overheard Mona and Mr. Raymond speaking French and although she had not heard the whole conversation she did hear the words *ce soir,* as Mona was leaving the office. Surprise and interest spread over her like a flush.

※

"Mona moaning," Cathy said during their break the following morning. She was a tall blonde woman in her early thirties who usually spent the break complaining about her husband or the woman who babysat her three-year-old son. She ripped the packet of sugar, put it in her cup and stirred the tea with a plastic stick. "God what an image, the two of them, like two cold fish slapping against each other."

"Yeah," in light of the ill-tempered interest Cathy showed, Amy wished she had not said anything. "Stupid really, just a dream."

※

The next evening when Amy was once again sitting on the mattress watching television, she heard a knock at the door. Inside the circle of the peephole, pressed close to her eye, were two men she had seen in the elevator. She called through the door. "Yes?"

"Hi, there. We were wondering if you have a newspaper we could borrow."

Remembering this moment, many years later, Amy felt a spontaneous sympathy for the girl she had been then, standing at the door, barefoot, stretching to see into the hall, for these were the first words the man who would become her husband spoke to her. She had a choice here; she knew that she could say that she did not have a newspaper or she could open the door and give the men the paper she had bought by the bus stop on her way home.

When she opened to them and they saw the sparse room, the taller man, the man who would be her brother-in-law said, "Guess you just moved in, eh?" and Amy explained how she usually lived on the main floor. And so this is how Amy's life with Philip began, with him stopping to get the paper every night, even after she moved back to the first floor. In stages these meetings grew into weekends spent together when they were introduced to each other's relatives and friends, weeknights cooking dinner, watching television and the new sensation of sleeping with someone every night. Amy continued her trips to and from the office, seeing the same commuters, the same men congregating in the cafeteria in their dark suits, like crows gathering in fields. And she saw Mona with them, dressed in a tailored suit, sitting quietly, listening to the men, the plain, flat shoes she wore because she was tall, the shy, compliant way she sat on the edge of her seat, sipping coffee.

Rumours began shortly after the flood when a co-worker saw Mr. Raymond and Mona holding hands in his office and someone else caught them on a Friday night on Bank Street walking arm-in-arm. "You may have been right," Cathy said as she and Amy worked at the long sorting table in the outer office.

"Leave them be, Cathy."

"That's right. You're in love now, so the world should be in love." She turned back to the job of sorting invoices.

Amy too went back to concentrating on the task before her. The night before when she woke she'd curled into the warmth of Philip's body and this is the memory that surfaced at that moment as she watched Cathy's hands shifting through the envelopes and paper in front of them. Amy was planning a move from the city to the small town where Philip had grown up, and their evenings were often full of people she had just met, people who would become her family, friends or neighbours.

Within a year of marrying, she became pregnant and gave up her job in the city. What she remembered best from the winter her son was born was rocking him to sleep while watching the snow fall into her yard. She had never known such peace, it settled in her slowly, falling like the snow, making her sleepy, warm and full. When her son was one year old and could be minded, Amy began work in a bookstore on the main street of the town. She enjoyed the work, the chatter between the women she worked with, and the way the sun lay in bands, stretching into the store from the front window in dusty rays during long afternoons, winter or summer. There was a calmness and natural rhythm to the work, an acceptance she never felt in her job at the office. She came to love the way the street changed throughout the day, when evenings drifted into the side lanes, or sun broke through the lace of leaves and fell into pieces of pure light. Many evenings she walked home from the bookstore, as the sky above her shimmered blue, and the houses crowded the streets with their dark, matronly bulk. The people she'd meet walking along the sidewalk, she greeted by name. Reaching the veranda of her home, she looked at the sky, dark then, like a scarf of deep indigo silk over the houses, held in place by the diamond pins of stars.

※

The winter Thomas turned eighteen, during his last year of high school, Philip told Amy he had fallen in love with someone in his office. It was a starkly cold day, and as he spoke she heard the wind rattling the dining room window. Her attention kept returning to the sound, even though she knew what he was saying was crucial, or perhaps she focused on the banging because what he was saying was too painful and, after the years of mounting indifference between them, too real. After Philip left, days went by when she'd forget to eat, when she lay on the sofa and be lost in the noise from the street: children, cars, dogs, common sounds that now excluded her. At times she slept soundly without dreams, but always the thought of Philip's leaving awaited at the rim of sleep, jarring her with its cruel insistence; she'd curl around it, as if it would burst from her, a snarl of pain, a tragic birth.

※

Living in the city three years later and once again working for a government department, Amy was waiting for a bus when she saw someone who looked familiar. The woman had a gaunt appearance, tall and thin and after a moment of watching her stand stiffly looking out to the street, Amy said, "Is that you, Mona?" And Mona turned with a smile.

"Yes," she said, her expression puzzled.

"It's me, Amy, remember we worked together." They were standing out of the wind in a doorway of a department store on Rideau Street. Within a few minutes of speaking Amy discovered Mona had left the office they shared a few years after Amy herself left and that she never married.

"That was a long time ago. My God, I haven't thought about that place in ages. Who did you work with again?"

"Mr. Raymond was my boss," Amy said and thought she saw a hardening of Mona's expression. A thin layer of grey had settled over Mona's face, giving her an aged, tired look.

"And you Amy? Any children?" Amy was telling her about her son when Mona's bus arrived and they quickened their conversation to hasty goodbyes. Shortly after, when Amy's bus appeared, she boarded and sat by the window. It was growing cold, a sad evening in October. As the bus moved toward the bridge, the neon of the city was replaced by streetlights and beyond, the darkness pooled around the apartment buildings and homes of Sandy Hill, streets where Amy's own mother had grown up.

She thought back to a time on another bus, when she was in her early twenties, coming home from her first job. She passed factories and fields, dark against the golden light of a setting sun. And from the vantage of more than twenty years she remembered the girl she'd been, sitting by the bus window, wondering what her life would hold in the years to come, as telephone poles, fences, and the whole wide landscape of bare fields pasted beneath a mottled sky slipped by her into the past.

WORST SNOWSTORM OF THE YEAR

My husband Philip found the stalled car when he was plowing a deserted stretch of road close to our village. It appeared through the blizzard like a mirage, covered in snow, a lumbering animal fast asleep. He'd told me, in the past, about finding people or dogs in distress while he was plowing, but this was the first time he'd come upon an accident. It looked like the car had simply veered off the road—there was no indication it had hit anything, no dead animal, or broken post, not even tracks, just a motionless car, snow covered, in the ditch. When he climbed down and cleared the windshield with his arm, Philip could hear his plow's engine idling like the uneven purr of a powerful animal.

An elderly woman and a younger man were in the front seat—Philip saw a line of blood on the woman's forehead and the man was moaning slightly but otherwise looked unharmed. There was something vulnerable in the silent way they were positioned side by side, as if sleeping, so that his first inclination was to turn away. Before heading back to the plow to call for help, he heard the woman moan and when he looked back she'd opened her eyes and was moving her mouth to speak, but she made no sound.

In the sixties she'd been a star, a comedienne who appeared on television shows featuring singing puppets and acrobats. Her thin legs beneath a dress which flared above her knees and her blonde hair teased high on her head made her look like a ludicrous doll. She squinted as she spoke and then opened her eyes wide to listen, puffing on a cigarette through a long holder while the audience laughed.

A decade later, when there were no longer variety shows that fit her type of humour, her popularity fell so that she was forced to play smaller venues or open for more popular comics. She divorced her husband, changed to a more tailored look—trousers and satin blouses—and flattened her hair, letting it return to its natural dark colour. Her look and single lifestyle provided new material, and she now portrayed her ex-husband as not only buffoonish, but also stupid and malicious. She was invited to appear on afternoon talk shows and comedy revues, but as the years went by and these venues dried up, her son, who was now her manager, arranged for a full agenda of work in community centers and dinner clubs. She preferred Florida where it was warm and the seniors remembered her, but she performed throughout the United States and into Canada. That was why in the winter of 1996, when she was in her mid-seventies, during the worst snowstorm of the year, she found herself in a ditch one Saturday evening on a back road between Ottawa and Toronto, close to the small town where I lived.

Typical of villages and towns in the area, the main street was predominantly stone and red brick Georgian buildings with white shutters that accented windows displaying candlesticks, wall hangings and decorative throws. Within the previous ten years, in an attempt to entice tourists, the older buildings in the town's core had been turned into gift shops and restaurants. At the end of the main street where the two central roads of the town met, there was a grey stone building that until sixty years ago had been a working mill. In summer, when visitors walked along the main street, they could feel the mist from the falls on their skin, and smell the churning water, a musty smell like the inside of cellars or other abandoned rooms. Most of the buildings in town were newer and less elaborate than those of the main street—there were clapboard houses and duplexes and bungalows with a mixture of siding and stucco.

Our house was red brick, small but with a large back yard. On the front lawn was a sign we bought the year we were married, shortly after we moved from the city. It had our names, *Amy and Philip Graves*, painted on it in green, and in the summer, marigolds and creeping white phlox grew beneath it, a flowerbed of white and gold that did nothing to uncover the complex moods and growing silence of our house. When I'd hear the sign squeaking from the living room I knew the wind outside had picked up, that a storm was on its way.

A few years after we moved here, we built a large porch on the front and a sunroom on the back. When I wasn't working at the bookstore—I spent most of my work days sitting on a high stool reading—I often sat in the sunroom, crocheting or doing needlework, and in winter watching the wind arrange the snow into shapes like large white stones smoothed by years of flowing water.

By the winter of 1995, I had lived in this house over nineteen years. Thomas, my son, who'd been born here eighteen years earlier, was finishing high school and anxious to move away. Often during dinner he'd be silent, and when his gaze would move to the window I knew he was thinking about his future, which university he'd attend and what he'd find there.

The afternoon of the cold day in February when the comedienne had her accident, I stood by the window, peeling turnips for dinner and watching the sky change from icy blue to navy above yards of pale mauve snow. I felt a chill and wrapped my sweater, which hung loosely from my shoulders, around me. After I had finished preparing dinner, a light snow began to fall and I called to my husband, "Looks like it's starting." Philip worked for the township and during the winter he was one of the crews that cleared the roads and highway. I knew soon he would dress in his work clothes and boots and drive his truck the half mile to the municipal compound—also the police and fire station—mount the plow enclosed in the pen behind the building, and begin clearing the snow. When the storm was extreme, it was difficult to see where the turns or laneways were, his only indication being the cone-shaped glow of the street lamps.

While he was out on the back roads, Thomas and I ate the dinner I had prepared that afternoon—roast pork, potatoes, turnips, with apple pie for dessert. We sat at the dining room table, as was our Sunday custom and, while Philip, whose chair sat empty, was descending the back road that led to the comedienne and her son, Thomas and I discussed his plans for the fall.

"I'd really prefer to go to Toronto; the program is the best in the country." He'd applied at both the university in Toronto and Edmonton and would hear shortly where he was accepted. He ate quickly, distractedly, and interrupted our conversation once to answer the phone. "I'm eating right now, call you back in ten," he said in a rushed voice. When he left the table I took our plates to the kitchen and looked through the window at the back yard now obscured by the storm—trees, the fences, even the weirdly lit pinkish sky, all erased by the snow.

)(

My husband told me about finding the comedienne and her son in their car when he returned home early the next morning. We were sitting at the kitchen table, drinking coffee, his hand around the mug for its warmth, dressed still in his work clothes because he'd be leaving again shortly. Snow crusted in the creases of his trousers and jacket melted slowly as he spoke in a contemplative way about how the white of the blizzard was blinding and when he finally came across the car, he had difficulty seeing it against the snow. "So what did you do?" I asked.

"What else could I do—I went to the plow, called for an ambulance and kept on plowing so they could get to the hospital."

When a doctor saw the comedienne, he determined she had a concussion, and they recommended she stay for tests. One of her first requests was to meet the man who'd found and helped them to reach the hospital. Philip asked me to join him and then suggested that rather than take the truck we walk.

The comedienne was in a single room propped on a pillow, wearing the pink satin sleeping jacket she'd insisted her son retrieve from the car—the Lincoln being repaired at the local garage. Her skin had a soft powdery look, dullish, but her eyes were bright and wet. "Sit over here, my dear," she said to me, pointing to the chair closest to her. Her hands, knotted with veins, were propped on her stomach.

"Well, first," she said, "I want to thank you for what you did for me and my boy, here," she lifted her hand and took hold of the cuff of her son's jacket. He smiled down without moving his head. He was tall, with thick dark hair, dressed in a tweed jacket, and his silence seemed less a sign of shyness or reticence than of boredom.

"I was only doing my job," Philip said.

She responded, "Well, even so, you do your job well." She finished by saying, "If you're ever in LA, come and see me. I have a big house where I live alone, now that my son is married, and I love visitors."

I said I'd like that, although I knew it was unlikely we would ever visit Los Angeles.

We smiled at each other with apparently nothing left to say, until the comedienne said quickly to Philip, "You look like my ex." She turned to her son. "Doesn't he look like your dad?" Her son grimaced, which could have meant he agreed or that he simply didn't care. "Don't take this wrong, he was a good-looking man when he was your age. It was later when he turned into a slug that he lost some of his charm."

Her son said the first words I'd heard him speak, "You don't have to do your routine now, Mother," and left the room.

"Do you have children?" she asked, not waiting for a reply. "It's best to kill them at around ten before they become so much smarter than you."

"He's eighteen," I said.

"Too late," She moved herself up on one arm. "Well good, now he's gone I can smoke, over there, under the sweater, there's a pack."

I found it and Philip said, "Do you think that's a good idea?" She smiled at me and said, "Men and kids," and I laughed.

※

"Well, that was fun," I said when we were walking home. Philip was not listening to me instead he was staring at the road. "Don't you agree? I mean she didn't have to ask to see you." He didn't answer.

I was forty-one years old and wore my hair short, honey brown with blonde streaks, a recent change, recommended by my hairdresser. My eyes were brown; I was five feet, four inches, and I had an overlapping front tooth, which I hated. Philip was forty-five and balding—something I never mentioned to him. He wore a beard, was average height and thin. I say these things now because I want you to see us on the road walking home, a man in jeans, a beige winter coat, the woman wearing a duffel coat, black trousers and a beige toque. It was cold and I want you to see the white of our breath when we spoke and to hear the way the snow beneath us, hard as marble, squeaked when we walked. I want you to notice how the man stares ahead through the cold and how the woman turns every few minutes to look at him.

I had often walked on this street on my way to or from work, but walking beside Philip on this day felt different. His silence, his refusal to look at me, added to the coldness in the air. When we arrived at our home with the door closed behind us, I asked, "What's wrong?" giving voice to a dread that had been growing for longer than I could bear to admit.

After he answered my question, I went upstairs to our bedroom and a while later he left the house. I heard the door close. There's a mistaken idea that the absence of sound cannot be heard, but after Philip left it was all I could hear, as I lay in bed, the blankets to my chin, rocking slightly.

※

After Thomas had left for school the next morning, to escape the silence I decided to visit the comedienne. It was a whim. When she had asked me to drop by, I had no intention of taking her up on the invitation. On my walk to the hospital, the stiff white landscape lay on either side of the road and the clouds were thin wisps before a durable blue sky.

"Well, how nice," the comedienne said when she saw me. I asked about the hospital, if she was being treated well but she did not respond. Instead she looked at me with a shrewd expression and said, "There's something wrong." I looked at the floor, at the tiles, the grout around each square and the metal rungs at the side of her bed. I knew she was watching me but I couldn't meet her eyes.

"You know my husband and I separated when I lost my job. He couldn't handle that I was no longer popular," she said, smoothing the blanket that lay over her, and then looking at me. "I could see something when you visited yesterday, a distance between the two of you. I noticed it."

"He wants to leave," I said after a moment silence. "He's met someone where he works. He said we haven't talked for years, and apparently he can talk to this woman." When I looked up I noticed the pale blue of her eyes, and a settled kind of resolve in them, almost like an illness.

⋈

The comedienne had begun her life as a daughter among seven daughters in a poor family, supported by her father's job as a butcher in a small town in Michigan. She told me about her sisters who never came to see her perform and with whom she had lost touch over the years. At twenty she met her husband, when she was working as a secretary, and within two years they married and had their first child. Her husband worked on the assembly line of one of the large car companies until he was forced to quit his job because of an accident, and the comedienne in turn was forced to find work. She began at a radio station as office manager, then producer and, not long after, hosted her own show. In 1962 she moved to TV, performing on variety shows and then movies where she'd play the maid or next-door neighbour. I saw one of her movies when I was young—in it she was the kooky friend of the heroine's mother and wore a fierce magenta wig that looked like bedroom slippers tufted around her head. She spent the movie spying on the main actors, then gossiping about them to her bored husband.

⋈

While she was hospitalized, I visited the comedienne every day, either before or after working at the bookstore where I had a part-time job. On the last morning when I arrived, I found her in bed, the television on mute, while out her window a light snow was falling. When she saw me, she said, "Doesn't it do anything around here but snow?"

"Not much else," I said and sat beside her on the bed. She told me about the snowstorms when she was growing up, about her sisters and parents and as she talked she laughed about everything, even things—like her estrangement from her sisters—I thought were sad. She called her husband "a goon," her first agent, a "blood-sucking serpent," and when she spoke about a famous actress she'd worked with, she referred to her as "a complete waste of boobs".

After an hour during which I smiled, laughed and listened, she stopped without warning and said, "It was awful when everything fell apart, that was in the early seventies—when suddenly I was no longer funny, but what really bothered me was the way my husband took it. He stopped talking to me and started spending his days in front the television."

I told her then when she grew quiet, looking away from me, that I kept seeing Philip the way he was on the night when he found her and her son on the back road. I would never know if what I imagined about that night actually happened, there was no way I could, but I did know how clearly I imagined it. He was in the glassed-in cab of the plow in the midst of the storm, carving a trail through the snow, a blanketed silence settling, disturbed only by the noise from the engine and the blades. And now when I thought of him there, I knew his thoughts would have been about the woman he'd fallen in love with, not his life with me and Thomas. He'd be thinking of the way she looked at her desk, the idle chatter, their shared smiles. She would have been the light in his mind he could not resist, a light where once there was only the dark monotony of his routine. And then I'd think about how I existed for him: the wife, the slippered, shuffling wife, with the sleepy look and worn nightgown, making coffee. "How did this happen?" I asked the comedienne. "How did I become this person?"

"You know, I remember very little about the accident except for your husband looking at us through the window. It seemed he stood there a long time and his face had a look on it—a kind of, what? What would you call it? A kind of wonder or maybe it was fear," she said. "But I knew that this man was going to help us, that everything would be all right."

Until that moment I'd been reluctant to recall the conversation with Philip before he left, but now I thought of him sitting at the dining room table. He still had his boots on and the snow was melting on the oriental carpet, he held his hat in his hand, lifting it for emphasis as he spoke. And the words he said made me realize the power of language to hold truth or betrayal, that those words alone were enough to shatter everything I'd come to rely on.

"I was surprised," I said, "that a life could be so quickly altered. One day it's fine, and the next everything's different." I continued, "Actually I've been thinking that maybe I walked away a long time ago. Philip always seemed as if he wanted to be alone and then there was Tom, his hockey, and school stuff. I know I went ages when I hardly thought about Philip in any real way." I picked at some lint on my trousers. "My life was pretty full and it's not like we weren't there, living together, fixing the house up, you know. I always thought of us as a team."

Night was moving in and the snowfall, which had been light when I arrived, was now thick. When I rose to leave she said, "So, maybe in the long run you got what you wanted?"

"It's a strange thing to think, but it would make it easier, wouldn't it, if I could believe that." And I remembered the morning after Philip left, I had laid in bed with the blankets flowed over me in soft curves like snow caught in yards and beneath I felt my body stir as I imagined spring stirred under the cold.

She smoothed the sheet and said, "I should tell you I'm probably leaving soon. My son wants me to go home, see my own doctor. I think he doesn't trust them here."

How small she was, surely no more than five feet, with circles of rouge on her cheeks like a doll, and her eyes made up with blue shadow. "Well, I hope I see you again before you leave," I said.

※

But I did not see her again. When I came the next day, she was gone. At the nurse's station they said she'd left that morning, that she signed herself out or rather that her son made her sign herself out. "Oh yes," I said. "She said she might leave so that she could visit her own doctor in California."

The nurse looked up at me and said, "Or perhaps her son didn't like what we found."

On the street alone, I tucked my chin against the cold into the scarf around my neck and listened to the huge sound of my trudging through the snow. I was following the route I walked with Philip the day he told me he was leaving. Here were the same fields of encrusted snow over bent cornstalks, the same distant trees on the horizon, a line of grey, like smudged charcoal, and then a wind that swept across the field, assaulting me with renewed cold. I wondered what the nurse meant, but when I arrived home I stopped thinking about the hospital or the comedienne, when my son met me at the front door. He was angry. "I didn't know he was gone," he said. "Why didn't you tell me?"

I put my arms around him and he shrugged me off. He went upstairs and I walked between the downstairs rooms hugging myself, ending up in the sunroom. It was still snowing, and I remembered how I'd rocked Thomas to sleep there the winter he was born, when it made me feel strong to know I was where I belonged.

Philip told me two months later, during one of our strained meetings, that he had heard on the radio on the way to meet me that the comedienne had died that day in Los Angeles. We were sitting in a restaurant not far from our home discussing how we would divide our belongings and how long to wait before selling the house. I looked at him for the first time since sitting down. "It was some kind of heart problem," he said. His face sagged and he kept his eyes averted, watching his hands in front of him on the table. When I didn't respond he said, "I heard you went to see her a few times when she was in the hospital," lifting his eyes to my face. Despite myself I felt sorry for him until he said, "What in the world would the two of you have to talk about?"

I did not answer him; instead I had an image of the comedienne when she was a young woman, standing by the sliding door of her home in Los Angeles. It was a house she'd told me about and I was surprised by how clear my image of her there was. She was staring into the yard, her head tilted back as she smoked. She could see her son with his friends lounging around the pool's aqua calm in the brilliant sun, and, at that moment, her husband came up behind her to kiss her ear, and I thought, *you take happiness in whatever fleeting form it presents itself.*

"It was strange when I saw her in the car that night," Philip said. "She was so white, and I thought, well, I thought she was dead, and it made me think how weird everything is." He became quiet and looked back at his hands as I looked out the window and wondered what the comedienne and her son had been discussing before the accident—the next show? Her new routine? Perhaps she glanced over at the speedometer and thought her son was driving too fast, that the snow was blinding, that she didn't know where she was, and felt caught in the careening car that torpedoed through the dense white of a snowstorm, and then her disbelief and surprise in that suspended moment just before the crash.

A NASTY BIT OF BUSINESS

I

In 1939 my husband and I sailed from London to New York on the Queen Mary. I think of that trip now, when I am at that point of life with so much behind and so little ahead that I am flooded with memory and a new sense of longing, not only for the time but for the woman I was then. And for my husband, for the union of us: Frances and Alec. At the time we'd been married for fifteen years, and it was to celebrate that we'd initially decided to take the trip. As we neared the harbour, I went on deck, leaving Alec alone in our stateroom. There I stood in the mist as the Statue of Liberty appeared through the fog, heavy and brooding, and later, behind the uneven edifices lining the shore, the Empire State building loomed over the skyline. I wore high heels and a full-length mink coat, a hat snug over my tight blonde curls. I knew I was attractive, although I'd have much rather been beautiful in that extravagant way some women are beautiful: "attractive" denotes effort. But that's what people would say if they saw me standing there, attractive and obviously wealthy.

This was the year Germany invaded Poland, a year of fear and uncertainty, another reason we had decided on this voyage, to escape the oppressive mood of Europe and, we reasoned, where better to go than New York, to see the World's Fair, breath in the city's bustle and promise for the future. Yet this was not what I was thinking as I stood watching the buildings crowd the shore. I felt safe in the fog, hidden, as I contemplated how my life, a life of privilege and entitlement, was built on deceit; the buildings I saw moving slowly by, indistinct in the fog, those buildings that stood as monuments to fortitude and progress, I knew, mirrored my own determination and resilience.

II

Amy closed her eyes, stretched her neck and used a finger to mark her place in the leather-bound book, a book she had discovered the week before in an antiquarian shop in Athens and, surprised to find it written in English, had included it in her purchases. The store had been a mess of strewn books and old bookcases stacked in no particular order, with items procured through bankruptcy or estate sales, discarded when people moved or died. Burrowed into the mounds of books and papers, the owner of the store, who sat near the front door, told Amy in tentative English that there were many keepsakes and jewellery in the back room, and journals and notebooks throughout the store that might interest her. She spent the best part of an afternoon rummaging through the disarray, leaving the store with five books, this journal among them, and an old pin with silver filigree and a small, scarlet red ruby. When she first saw the brooch she lit upon it; the silver was tarnished but the gem gleamed like a hidden tear of blood. She was wearing it on the day she began reading the old journal. Only twenty or so pages were written upon and the handwriting had elongated spikes for the "p"'s and "f"'s, giving the text a formal appearance and yet, ever consistent, it moved along smugly, with an obvious rhythm and sense of itself.

Reading the first page, Amy imagined the buildings of New York through the fog-like shapes of smudged pencil lead, and she saw the woman standing on the deck also washed in the same smoky light, although she'd never been on an ocean liner, had never even been to New York. She was reading the book at a beachside restaurant in Chania on the island of Crete, lifting her eyes on occasion to a view of the shore and the sky. When she'd arrived at the restaurant, the waiter welcomed her with a wide smile and a greeting, and then seated her at a table close to the shore, bringing a small plate of anchovies with the menu. She ordered lunch, a mixed seafood grill, and sat reading, alone at the table, glancing up at times to look at the people strolling by on the beach and the miraculous blue of the sea beyond.

The woman in the journal reminded Amy of her aunt Margaret, a woman of means, as her mother would have said, a woman who married well and was always surrounded by evidence of this lucky turn of events. But Amy was trying not to think of her family, or her home back in Canada. She had come to Greece as a retreat more than a holiday, a way to show herself she could travel and enjoy life alone. Life alone was what waited for her back home. In the past six months she had been left by her husband, who was living with another woman and this woman's child in the small town where Amy and he had lived for almost twenty years. And her son had gone just weeks before to begin university in Edmonton. The fact that her marriage was over followed her like a high whining sound and was the background to all she did and all she thought. She found that when she went through her day, showering or drinking coffee on the balcony of her hotel, her thoughts would drift back to the town where she had lived and the house that she had shared with her husband and son.

She was grateful for the diversion of the journal, grateful to be able to imagine this woman dressed in her stylish clothes, in the midst of other passengers grouped on the deck, with the famous skyline sliding by. Perhaps because the voice reminded her of her aunt Margaret, Amy could see clearly the way Frances walked, with short clipped steps, or how she'd enter a room taking off her gloves one finger at a time and then folding them into her palm, because this was the kind of mannerism Amy remembered her mother and her mother's sisters having.

III

My first night in Manhattan I lay beside my husband as he slept and breathed in the evening air full of the sounds of the city, of traffic and voices from the street ten floors below, where darkness was pushed aside by the rush of passersby. It was an impressive room of brocade curtains, thick mouldings and marble floors, like my life at the time, heavy with decorum. I could see the white-veined moon between the curtains like a silk circle caught in the sky. My husband slept as if there was nothing to wake him, no stain on the silk circle of his soul. Only I knew better.

He rolled over, moaned in his sleep. At times I wished I could follow him down the narrow alleyways of his dreams. What would I find there? Perhaps the couple who raised him, people I'd never met, but who in their simplicity I imagined as slack-jawed with worn red hands. Or was it the face of the Greek farmer who could not understand Alec's excited words? Our room was very still, very dark, except where the hall light gathered beneath the door and glowed like the line at the horizon the moment after the sun descends.

We had a house in England, my husband's house, but I wanted to sell it and spend our life travelling and living in rented villas or hotels. It was a change I contemplated after the last time I stood outside the dining room of that old house and overhead the servants speaking. "She's a different sort, that one," said a maid named Alice, who had worked in the house since she was a child. "I'll say," another servant, a younger woman, said. "And I'm not sure about that nasty bit of business a few years ago; the explanation seemed just a little too convenient." As I listened I thought how old and soiled the house had become, with its memories and history and the percolating mean-spirited gossip and suspicion, and so I convinced Alec to sell it and we began our travels across Europe and America.

We'd arrive at resorts and hotels with heavy trunks marked with the places where we'd been: Venice, Nice, Monaco; we'd be dressed to the teeth, sable coats, and elaborate hats, dramatic as the plumes of foolish birds; my hair in finger waves and Alec in spats, a fedora, a coat flung over one arm, a hand grasping a cigarette holder. How grand we were, and incomprehensible.

IV

The Hotel Panorama sat on a steep hill, and from Amy's room, beyond the coast highway and low rise buildings, provided vast views of the Cretan Sea. Behind the hotel were unruly olive groves that stretched across the mounting terrain, its villas like stark white stones in the sun. Amy walked along the pathways through the fields during the late afternoon, passing bushes of wild geraniums and bougainvilleas that glowed a bright, fierce red.

She'd always been a person who enjoyed habit and shortly after arriving in Chania, she found a restaurant across the street from the hotel that looked out on the sea, where she was treated with the appropriate mixture of courtesy and neglect, so that during her stay it became her favourite place to eat. Sometimes that was all she did in a day other than read and walk the steep paths along the hills.

After she'd eat lunch, she watched the tide and the children play in the sand, the tourists walking by, some holding hands, and she read from the books she brought in her canvas bag, a bulky novel translated from the French, a collection of poetry, a book of short stories, but always saving for last the story about Frances and Alec. One afternoon the waiter, a young handsome man of about twenty, approached her. "Beautiful day," he said and twisted his head to see what she was reading. "What do you have there?" Perhaps because he was the same age as her son, Amy felt warmly toward him, and she responded "Oh this, a journal I bought in Athens or it's a notebook, I'm not quite sure." This answer seemed to please him and he walked back to the kitchen humming.

During the following days she learnt that his name was Costa, that his brother owned the restaurant, and that he was hoping to earn enough to be able to become part owner. He would smile when he saw her approach the tables closest to the beach, their blue and white striped umbrellas flapping, and say "good day, reader-lady." The greeting was like all of his English, a little stilted, and yet Amy found it endearing.

V

Let me return to a point shortly after the war, in 1920, to a time when I was poor, when I was attending university on a scholarship, because you see I was clever, and my parents were dead. They died when I was a young teenager, and I moved in with a maiden aunt, the sister of my father in a house in Beacon Hill in the heart of Boston. This aunt was used to a solitary life and left me to my own devices, which were mainly reading and sketching. I spent most of my time alone walking the streets close to our home, or reading in the library. You'd think that all those calm hours of study would have created in me a love of serenity, for pursuits of the mind, but you'd be wrong, for in my heart I was wild and raging, desperate to escape. My aunt's kindness, which everyone who knew her thought was the overriding quality of her character, always seemed to me to be a form of stupidity, ineptitude at its worst. The way she'd search out abandoned cats and dogs to feed made me think her an idiot and so I retreated into books, a sanctioned activity that meant she never expected me to help with housework or any of her charitable pursuits. I was a sensible-looking girl, with short thin blonde hair around a sharp-featured face; usually I wore walking shoes and my school uniform, even on weekends.

I'm giving too much detail here; it's enough to say my cleverness (it was never more than that) won a scholarship for me to attend a prestigious university in Britain and made my aunt irrationally proud. When she invited her friends and some of the neighbours to celebrate, they crowded into her orderly home, and their presence filled the rooms with a sycophantic eagerness. One neighbour in particular, a man who I'd always tried to avoid, followed me, grinning an obsequious grin, and after every sentence he uttered, he'd snort, so that by the end of the evening I could barely contain my impulse to poke his face with something sharp.

My first year at university, I met a wealthy girl whose father was a shipping magnate. She grew up in the type of house I associated with murder mysteries, large rooms with heavy furniture, mouldings and drapery. Being clever, perhaps even conniving, I ingratiated myself to her, and as so many of the other girls were jealous or could not abide her attitude of superiority, we became best of friends. I knew this was possible only because I deferred to her on most every subject and because I wrote her term papers while she'd go dancing with men who studied at a nearby university. I should mention she was beautiful, with long auburn hair and green eyes. Can you imagine how that made me feel? This tall, graceful creature, with the most stylish clothes—they were her true loves: clothes and shoes—who fascinated men with her flamboyance, standing beside me, the church mouse, as I heard myself referred to by the other girls in the dormitory. I hated her, plain and simple. I hated her with an energy that ran through me like a hidden glacial stream, endless and pure. And still, despite the icy current of disdain I felt for her, for everything she represented, we became inseparable during those years at university.

I am racing over the facts of my life when I was young, but of course you know there was an intensity and repetition to the routine of those years; there were nights in my room when the evening sunk into the courtyard outside and when the moon rose and days when sun stretched in long fingers of light into the library where I spent hours reading. You know all this because you know how life happens in a series of patterns and repetitions, of days and months and years, so I will only tell you that I and this woman—Stephanie was her name—became friends and you can fill in the depth of this friendship: in classrooms, walking along the arboured crossways on campus, driving in her car and even spending holidays with her father, where we ate in a dining room so large my aunt's entire house could easily have fit inside.

I think back on these days and wonder how I was different then than I am today. It was the last period of my life that I was without culpability, when I could not assign the darkness of my drives, my desires, to a deed, to a devious plan.

Stephanie fell in love—of course there were many boys, then men, who were interested in her, but this man was different, a poet on a scholarship. He was exactly the type of man Stephanie's father feared she would choose to marry and perhaps this was part of his attraction but, as in most things, she was adamant. She would marry him, and it would be the largest wedding in years, in a family noted for conspicuous shows of extravagance.

Her father called me to his office. The walls were lined with walnut bookcases and there was a smell of varnish and something pungent, acidic, lemons perhaps. I tried to identify the scent as I sat waiting for him. When he arrived—a thin man with grey hair and a long drawn face—he said, "Tell me, Frances, about this man," and I told him what I knew, which was not much more than he knew. Then Stephanie's father said without looking at me, "He will never make her happy; he will not know how to deal with her, to please her." I agreed, but we both knew there was nothing we could do to change her mind. "I'm glad we had this chance to speak," he said, rising, "and I guess the next time I'll see you will be at the wedding." But it was not to be, because as fate would have it, he died two days later of a heart attack, postponing the marriage by two months.

With her father's death, Stephanie was now an even wealthier woman, and her attitude changed to reflect her new status. She spoke in a more authoritarian tone to the servants and became increasingly demanding about food preparation, how the table was set, the rooms cleaned. At the wedding I stood for her. Let me stop here for a moment to tell you about that day because it was exceptional. She was dressed in a white lace gown with pearls sewn into the back seam for buttons. She wore a veil over her dark hair and her eyes shone so bright, with such beauty. She was still the same demanding, self-concerned woman, but on that day her happiness was real, it surrounded her, and touched all of us who were there. Her groom, who never left her side, was handsome, blond, tall, and, already at his young age and despite his lack of position, a pleasant, witty conversationalist.

VI

At this point in the reading of the story, Costa surprised Amy by sitting down at the table before her. He was curious about what she was reading, the selection of old books she brought every day and placed on the table, alternating between them and glancing up to look at the sea. He said, "Not as busy today... a good day to sit in sun."

"Yes, a beautiful day."

It felt strange to Amy to speak with him after the days of bright quiet and nights of dreamless sleep where she simply drifted in and out of thoughts about her life, as if it were a room she could visit and abandon. A skinny dog, one Amy had seen before along the shore, that looked like a stray, came bounding into the restaurant from the beach, its tail and paws wet from running in the water.

"Ah, there's my dog," Costa said.

"He's so thin." Amy patted his head as he nuzzled her with his leathery nose. His fur felt warm under her hands. A couple came from the beach and stood on the patio and Costa rose from the table to seat them. The dog stayed by Amy's side, and after a few minutes, lay down and fell asleep under her table as she continued to read, and as she did, stopping on occasion to ponder what she was reading, she absent-mindedly stroked the dog so that under her hand she could feel his coat, now soft and cool in the shade.

VII

During the wedding reception, I smiled a lot and watched the crowd without saying much; I watched Stephanie's relatives drink and laugh, I listened to stories and felt envy so potent I was ill. Stephanie was a beautiful woman, I'd mentioned that, and together they were a beautiful couple with everything before them—trips to the continent, summers in villas by the Aegean or Adriatic, this was their future. And me? Well I would most likely become someone's secretary, a servant of sorts, my desires or my thoughts never sought. Stephanie herself had hinted at my taking up such a post in her house but I had not pursued the option. I remember watching her and her new husband leave, the wave of her white-gloved hand from the car and shouts of goodbye. They were to honeymoon at a resort on Santorini, a place she described as brilliant with sun and where light fell strong and full on the white of the sea walls and the villas. She was sitting in her bedroom as she discussed her plans with me and although she did not describe it in such detail—did I mention she was incapable of any true appreciation of anything beyond her physical self?—I could see it, glorious and full in the summer morning when the sunlight fell, sticky and warm as honey. I know now that these images are true because I have been there and felt such mornings, and the cool Aegean breeze at night.

Stephanie became bored in Santorini, that was the story. She wanted to see different scenery, and so her husband, woefully unsuited or unaccustomed to the whims of a rich, spoilt wife, decided to take her to Crete, to explore some of its outer reaches. She complained she'd been there and her husband said, "Ah, but not to the west coast to the incredible lookouts I've heard about, so remote you have to get there by foot."

Before I continue, there is something I need to share, something which may help to explain the disbelief I always felt about the possibility of happiness, something from my past which in my telling of this tale I glossed over. And that was that the facts surrounding my parents' death were in truth dramatic and a turning point in my life. I tell everyone it was a car accident—what other story can explain losing them on the same day?—when it was actually a murder suicide. My father, always a morose man, killed my mother with a kitchen mallet—hit her on the head, but in all fairness to him there was evidence of only one sharp blow. Just like her to fall dead at the first retribution for a lifetime of nagging. He in turn hanged himself. It was a Saturday and I came home from a friend's house in the late afternoon to find them both. That's when I went to live with my father's sister, who shared his reticence, but not his melancholic nature. And that's when I started to read and sketch in earnest, but I told you all this before. Some people where we lived felt sorry for me, but many more saw me, either secretly or when speaking candidly, as the offspring of two strange people, someone not to be trusted.

When I told Stephanie that my parents died in a car accident, she said "Really?" with blunt curiosity. Actually, I liked that about her, as I came to like the hatred she created in me, the way my duplicity felt like a secret I kept and gave definition to my very being. I liked too the bald way Stephanie would ask questions about the horrible things in life: accidental deaths, murders, abuses of any sort. If she hadn't been wealthy and trained to project a certain reserve, she would have loved the tabloids with their ghoulish coverage of the seedier aspects of the news. "So, did you get to see the bodies...I mean after?" I had never been asked this question and was not sure which lie to tell, so I just shook my head "no" in a closed way that made her think the memory was too painful to recount.

But where was I before I backtracked? Oh yes, Stephanie and her husband went to Crete, staying in the town of Chania at a hotel near the port.

VIII

Amy dropped the book. So they'd been here. Perhaps they drove by this very spot, on another warm, bright day, identical to the day she was sitting in; perhaps they passed this very shore and the sun was just as hot on their skin as it was on Amy's.

The day before Amy had visited the port, ate at an outdoor restaurant that looked out to the water, and shopped at one of the many shops that catered to tourists. She had bought a leather wallet for her son and a shawl for herself. How many years ago would Alec and Stephanie been here? And how many other people have moved through that town with its ancient buildings, cobblestones, and satiny water slapping the dock? During lunch Amy was aware of the teeming life that had for hundreds of years invaded the port and nearby streets, the constant wash of change, the families and stories, the intrigues and traumas. When Stephanie and her husband stayed there, no doubt they stayed in the most luxurious hotel, eating dinner out by the water, as the evening swept in like cool silk against skin. Looking out past the children, the commotion by the shore, Amy could imagine the two of them, tall and thin in pale linen; he'd be wearing a fedora and holding an ebony cane. It pleased her to think Stephanie would be wearing the brooch she'd found in Athens, that pin with its setting of silver and ruby, that caught the sun in a drop of red.

IX

There was a breeze off the sea that floated into their room at night, while Stephanie curled beside her husband and he looked into the dark, smoking cigarettes, thinking, a careless arm over his head. This is the image I created of their honeymoon nights, her swooning slumber and his dark contemplation of what his life would be from then on. Soon after arriving they decided to rent a car and drive to the furthest western point of the island, to the most rugged section of the coast. The car strained up the small dirt road that twisted along the line of the sea, as the sun fell on the churning water far below. The cloudless sky was a pale china blue. When they left the car to view the landscape, the sea looked like limitless fabric, laid out and moving as if beneath its surface a powerful animal thrashed. Stephanie raised her hand to protect her eyes from the glare.

You may wonder how I knew about the cliffs and that day, how I could see so clearly the sun, the mist rising from the sea. You see, I returned a few years later, to the very spot where they had stood. It was land that had not changed much in thousands of years, in spite of being assaulted continuously by wind.

You know what's going to happen, don't you? It's a common enough story, something you'd read in a novel. Of course the question through all this was: Why did he not love her? Why when he saw her face, so smooth and her eyes dark and shining, or when he saw her body, a gift she proffered, her breasts, her long legs, narrow waist, why was he not moved to love, not touched by her nakedness and beauty? And why—the most perplexing of questions—did he love me?

X

Amy put the journal down. There it was. What was unknown when she first encountered Frances standing on the deck of the ocean liner, looking out as the city slid by.

Costa came to her table and asked if she wanted anything else and Amy asked for a coffee. Over the past week, she had come to love the Cretan coffee which tasted so much like rich chocolate. She glanced at the shoreline as a group of children played in the surf with Costa's dog, which was barking and jumping at the waves. One of boys who was chasing the dog and laughing caught her attention, and she thought he looked like the boy who now lived with her husband. A coldness came over her, even though the day was warm, even though she was sitting before an idyllic scene, the blue sea, the flawless sky, the children and the playing dog. And she pulled her sweater around her, looked out squinting into the sun and back to the grounds remaining at the bottom of her cup, a muddy, bitter sludge.

XI

When he found the perfect spot, where only the glaring sun was witness, and where the cliff was sharp and high above the sea, he pushed her from behind, maintaining pressure as her shoes scuffed the loose rocks, until with a final shove she was gone. It was as if the air she fell through opened and shut behind her, so clean was her disappearance. He stood silent for a moment looking out at the sky, and then returned to the car, driving quickly to the nearest house, trying to explain to the farmer between gasps that his wife had fallen.

They never found the body, but she died there, I have no doubt. He told me how she tried to twist around to grab him but was unable, that her feet were off the ground and she was kicking stones over the cliff. He told me how moments before she had been laughing and running before him. He told me he did it for me, for us.

But I knew this, I knew what we would do for each other, what we had done, how I introduced them at the library, and how I told her about him, and coached him on how to interest her, what to say and how to not appear anxious. I'd tell her about his liaisons with other women to make her think he was unavailable, a condition Stephanie always found irresistible. I think she knew that I loved him and that piqued her interest further. I researched where the coastlines of Greece were the most rugged and steep.

I suppose he loved me because we were so much alike, we both spent our time among those people smiling and hating, and yet those people, as we thought of them, are who we are now. Quite the irony, that. Some people would say that living off of someone else's money, living well because of the deceit of our actions would lead to a life of regret and unhappiness. Don't believe them.

XII

"Costa, tell me this," Amy said during the last meal she would have in his restaurant. "What is the coastline like further west from here? I mean, are there any hotels or houses?"

"That is a funny question," he said, smiling. Another waiter was working in the restaurant on this day and Amy had noticed Costa's attention was diverted, that he was jumpy and anxious to seat people who approached the restaurant.

"Well," Amy said, "I read it was pretty rocky with cliffs and I just wondered if anyone has built there."

"It is dangerous, but very, very beautiful." A couple came to the seaside entrance and he left Amy to seat them and did not return for another ten minutes. She picked up one of the novels she kept in her bag, but her thoughts kept returning to Frances and Alec.

When Costa came back he said, "I want to build there someday."

"I was thinking of going to see it, of maybe renting a car," she said, "but my time here is coming to an end."

A patron called him over with a request and he left Amy. *He works hard*, she thought, *with little reward*. Looking back to her book she caught sight of the silver brooch; the ruby glinting blood red, the colour deeply beautiful, and she touched the gem with something akin to affection.

As she entered her hotel room the telephone was ringing, the first time since she arrived that it had rung. It was her husband calling from Canada, and she thought as he spoke how his voice had already lost some of its familiarity. He told her there were papers at the lawyer's office waiting for her signature and asked when she would return. She fingered the brooch and moved to the window.

After a moment of silence when Amy wondered if their connection had been lost, he said, "You know before Tom left for university, he wouldn't even meet my girlfriend."

"Well, that's his choice, isn't it?" Amy said and thought of her son the last time she'd seen him, how he shrugged off her embrace and told her not to worry about him alone in Edmonton. She moved the curtain to see the line of stores and restaurant across the boulevard where the children were still playing.

"I know, I know," he said. "It's hard, that's all." The dog joined the children, barking and running into the waves. "So, how is it there? As beautiful as you thought?"

Amy saw Costa emerge from the walkway by the side of the restaurant. He stretched, looked from side to side and seeing the dog, called him, slapping his thigh. She stepped closer to the window. A glare from a truck windshield flashed a sudden spear of light into the room that for a moment blinded Amy so that she turned her head away and said, "Oh yes, it's even more beautiful than I'd imagined."

TOADHEAD

The year I turned forty-nine, I lived alone in a house that had been built over a hundred years before, a large house, converted to small apartments. I'd lived there for almost seven years, the years after my marriage ended, when I moved back to Ottawa from the small town where my son was born and raised. My kitchen window looked out onto an alley and a courtyard with a disarray of rickety staircases, lawn chairs and clotheslines heavy with sheets and towels flapping wild in an inconstant wind.

I worked as an assistant to the communication department of a government research institute, and so Saturday or Sunday were the only days I could linger over a coffee and newspaper and watch the morning light enter the kitchen, a light that outside edged the fences, stairways and clotheslines, stitching the yard wall to wall. On the ground floor lived a woman not much younger than my mother and I'd see her sometimes sitting in a lazy-boy under the light of a floor lamp, the television on, and I wished it could be my own mother, who now lived in a nursing home where I visited most nights.

Although small, my living room had a working fireplace, and there were leaded glass panes in my dining room window, details that endeared the apartment to me and so over the years I grew very fond of the place. Where I worked, in contrast to my apartment, was a jumble of offices and labs off long hallways, stacked with files on cabinets, papers teetering on desks beside computers and lab benches, the rooms full of the sound of talk, of phones ringing and printers humming.

One morning, Irene, the receptionist, a woman who'd worked there for over twenty years and whose talk was propelled by twenty years of grievances, informed me by way of a yellow sticky note pasted on my door that I'd received a phone call. It turned out that the vaguely familiar name belonged to an old boyfriend, someone I met when I was thirteen and he sixteen. The day we met he'd worn a black leather jacket and smoke from the cigarette between his lips spiraled before his face and dirty blond hair. My mother had seen him in front of the house smoking and said she hoped he wasn't waiting for me, but by then I'd become expert at avoiding her, at escaping to my room upstairs where I'd dry my hair straight and apply black eye makeup and pink lipstick.

In broad strokes, during our phone conversation, I discovered what he'd been doing in the intervening years (investment banking, raising two children, living part of the year in a Florida condo) and as we spoke, Paul, a co-worker, appeared before me. He gestured if I'd like to join him for coffee, and I placed the phone against my shoulder and said, "This may take awhile, you better go without me."

"I'll pick you up at lunch then."

Paul lived in the suburbs, had lived there most of his adult life, with his wife and children. I learnt from our lunch conversation that his routine centered around Karen, his youngest child, and her assorted sports now that his other two children were at university.

The year before, at our Christmas party, I'd met his wife, a short, placid woman, with cropped grey hair, who spoke of her church group, and seemed to me unsuited to Paul. At work he was normally quiet but when he befriended you, as he had me, his talk became spiked with jokes and we often spent our breaks in humorous awe at the absurdity of our workplace and some of our co-workers.

A few hours later when Paul returned to my office, he said, "Who was on the phone?"

"An old boyfriend."

"And what does *he* want?"

"Who knows?"

"So, lunch?" Eating in the cafeteria meant taking an elevator to the basement and walking along hallways full of pipes, tubes and thick bands of wires, hallways that always reminded me of the inner workings of some mechanical and sloppy brain. Two women ran the cafeteria, which was one of a series for the campus where we worked, and they scurried behind the counters like obedient rodents wearing thick padded shoes and hair nets. Paul was one of their favourite clients and they'd often give him a cookie or muffin without charge when he teased them.

"Well, there she is," he said to the shorter of the two, a blonde woman in her late thirties who had a high bosom, stocky legs in white hose and a wide attractive smile, which she displayed after Paul spoke.

On our way to the table I said, "She has a huge crush on you, you know".

"You're nuts."

"And you like it, don't you? You like the attention." He put his tray on the table and when he smiled, I said, "It makes you pretty pathetic, you know."

The cafeteria was a large room with the kitchen at one end separated by blue and white metal dividers. Tables rimmed the room, one side had high windows that looked out, ground level, at the parking lot and the other wall had nondescript artwork on what looked like thick cardboard. The scenes of sailing ships on a blue sea, crashing waves on a shoreline, or a cabin in a forest had been there for years, certainly since I had started working there. All were splattered with food. "How is it possible that food gets on those god-awful paintings?" Paul said. "Do people fling it around? Or hit them with their spoons?"

"Possibly, or maybe it's when they vomit, you know it splashes up."

"You really have a weird imagination," he said. "People don't know that about you, they think you're sweet."

"Ask my ex-husband about that." The soup was thick as pudding and tasted like hot flour.

"So, how did you know that guy who called?"

"We grew up in the same neighbourhood."

"And you're going to meet him?" His look became intent and he held his fork over his plate, his foot bouncing on the brace of the chair beside him.

"For a drink, and maybe dinner."

One of the scientists with a lab close to my office sat down in the chair beside Paul. "Well I hope I made the right choice with this roast pork," he said. It was smothered by thick gravy that looked suspiciously like my soup.

A few nights later when I approached my old friend in the bar where we'd agreed to meet and he looked up from his drink, his expression was hooded and intense, as if I was a hunk of meat that had escaped, through folly or luck, the stab of his fork. I had only to see that expression once to know I would not meet him again. His self-congratulatory talk was suffocating and as I watched his mouth stretch into a wide smile and his eyes budge, I named him Toadhead. The next week he left roses with Irene, who brought them to my office when Paul was there and said, "I'm not really supposed to be a receptionist for personal deliveries, you know."

"What's this? An admirer?" Paul said.

"Oh God, it's from Toadhead," I said, opening the tiny envelope and reading the note, *To our impossible union.*

"Toadhead? That's what you call him?"

"Yeah."

"Nice."

"No, not really," I said.

"What do you mean?"

"Oh, I don't know, I guess I thought he'd be smarter, I certainly thought he'd be kinder." Paul was leaning against my desk, hitting his palm with a ruler, in feigned nonchalance.

"So, what about you, any plans for the weekend?" I asked.

"Karen has a hockey game but other than that I'm not sure. The usual I guess."

"I just wonder how that boy who'd been so funny could turn into such a jerk."

"What? Toadhead again?"

"Yeah, I was just thinking."

"You do that all the time, off on another topic before I can follow." But he was smiling and tapped my head with the ruler before leaving the office. Alone, I was left with the image of Toadhead, how when we left the bar to have dinner I looked down, saw his shoes and imagined the feet inside, fringed with crooked toes. He pulled my chair out and sat facing me. Perhaps the thought of his feet planted below us, flat as fish, or that I could still feel the grasp on my elbow as he steered me toward the table, spurred me, so that I said, "What the hell happened to you?"

"I understand, you're angry because I left you all those years ago," he said. "I can understand that." He lifted his hand to move my hair away from my face and I jerked back to avoid his touch.

※

When I went to see my mother at the nursing home the next day I told her about Toadhead to see if she remembered him and she said she recalled a boy who waited on the street for me, smoking cigarettes. "I thought you were too young for those shenanigans," she said. I had made us tea and she was sitting in the lazy-boy chair where she often fell asleep watching television. "There were always kids around," she said and then became thoughtful. "Oh, but you were the one, such a scamp." She looked up, meeting my eyes, "And secretive, so secretive. I never knew what you were thinking."

※

A cold March day, the year I was thirteen: I was in my bedroom and the boy who would become Toadhead started pitching rocks at my window. My mother called from the kitchen, "Amy, I think there's someone outside who wants to see you." I ran down the stairs and rushed to the front step, breathless to speak to him, to see what he was wearing and to hear what he would say. But today I wish I'd paused instead to look at my mother in the kitchen. Her dark hair would've been piled on her head and she'd be wearing an apron streaked with gravy over her skirt, having just arrived home from her job in an office downtown. And the kitchen, with its café curtains that she'd sewn, would have been warm with yellow light and smelled of the meatloaf she was cooking. If I had looked. If only I had looked. Her high heels were in the hallway and I kicked them out of the way to get to the door.

A month after meeting Toadhead there was a Christmas party at my office, and because I'd stayed to help with the clean up, I was one of the last to leave. There was still a sense of the forced gaiety of such an event and I could hear people in their offices, shutting down their computers and calling out their farewells. In the cafeteria, streamers swayed from the ceiling and the banner that stretched across the entrance drifted in a current of slow air. The hallway was dark and quiet, the rooms also, and despite how familiar those rooms were, they appeared in that moment to be foreign and brooding.

The darkness of night pressed against the window, making it a black mirror where I could see the assortment of office furniture and equipment, the clock on the wall, and my own image sitting behind the desk. I looked up and saw Paul enter the room. Filing cabinets blocked my direct view, so that I could only see him in the dark of the window. We stared at each other without speaking, until a few moments later he said, "I love you, I have since the first moment I saw you." He stared another moment while I stood, then he turned and left so that I was left to wonder if I'd imagined him there.

His car was gone when I passed the parking lot on the way to the bus stop. On the ride home I leaned against the window as we drove through the bitter night, stopping at traffic lights and to let people on and off. When I left the bus and walked to my apartment it began to snow so that the streetlights above the sidewalk glowed like orbs of frost. When I entered my apartment I stood for a moment in the dark, my back against the door, the sounds of the street settling into the space before me. When I turned the lamps on, the room that I'd created with its white sofa, sheer curtains, red Oriental rug, leaped out and calmed me with its promise of home.

⋇

"So, what did you do?" my mother said. She was feeling well, alert and interested in my story. A Sunday afternoon, between Christmas and New Year's, out her window cold stretched into the hard blue sky while the winter sun shone bright on the sill and wall behind her.

"Nothing. I did nothing. And I haven't seen him since."

"And what about that other guy, from the old neighbourhood?"

Ah, yes, Toadhead. "Yeah, he's gone."

At the end of the television show we were watching, when I got up to leave, she said, "I'll go with you." She pushed her walker before her, a folded cane and purse in its basket. "I'll tell you something. I think you care for him, that Paul person. I always did," she said at the door.

"Really?" I said. "That's good to know." I leaned to kiss her goodbye, straightened. *When had she become so small?* Pulling my coat around me, the day brittle with cold, I turned to face the street and breath in the icy air. Houses with frosted windows huddled in rows, with smoke steaming up from their chimneys. A sudden gust of wind hit me and I knew, with the same force and spontaneity as that wind, what I would say to Paul on Monday morning and what it would feel like to sit before him in his office, quiet, watching his face cloud with worry and then smooth into a grin, full of a dangerous and expensive joy.

VISITATIONS

I turned ninety last July and in November I was forced—by my family, by the doctor at the hospital, by the social worker in her crowded office, and by the worst, the saddest of truths—to move from my apartment to a residence for the elderly. The day of the move was blistery cold and I saw in its bitterness, in the pale, absent sky, a cruel omen. From my first day here, I haven't liked it and I haven't liked Sue, the woman who runs the place, who told me I must join the other residents for meals, that I haven't made an effort to adjust. *I've adjusted enough in my life*, I said. She folded her arms across her scrawny chest and said she would have to speak to my family about this defiant attitude—as if they don't already know.

Tonight my youngest daughter Amy visited; she sat on the end of the bed, fanned herself and said the heat of my room was oppressive. She is in her early fifties, divorced almost a decade, and divides her life between working in a government office and living alone in an apartment on the opposite side of the canal to the neighbourhood where I grew up. I watched her leave, clutching her coat closed, bracing herself against the cold February night. At the glass doors of the main entrance I saw her cross the street to her car, then turn, hesitate and wave. I waved back, then pushed my walker along the hall, my purse and room key in its basket, and returned to my room. I was restless during her visit, opening dresser drawers and cupboards. "What do you want, Mom?" she asked following me, but I did not answer. It's a good question though, *what do I want?*

)(

It gets dark early these days, before dinner. I hate eating anyway. I hate looking around at the mass of us in the dining room, the walkers and wheelchairs lining the walls and tables, the stoop of heads over tasteless soups and mounds of food the consistency of porridge. The darkness at the window reflects the room back, showing an alternate, darker landscape where these rooms are locked in their routine of meals and bingo.

When I lie in my room with my eyes closed, as I tend to do when I am not either eating or attending to my person, I return to the house on Nelson Street, where I lived as a child. I see the Sunday table set, a dinner of roast beef, Yorkshire pudding, roasted potatoes, and apple pies in the kitchen cooling for dessert. The smell of the food mingled with the smell of furniture polish and floor wax and mixed with noises from the roadway, or the conversations as members of my family took their seats. I was the youngest of four sisters and every night we'd sit in the same position around the dinner table. Closest to my father, sitting straight with wide shoulders was my oldest sister, Margaret, beside her Dorothy, who projected an aura of fragile grace, and beside me Rita, who was always distracted and usually speaking. On the other side of the table were three of my five brothers, who would take the opportunity of my father's distraction to punch each other. Martin, the oldest boy still at home, worked for a company that made coffins. As a wedding gift he'd made me a cedar chest, and in the years to come when I'd see its bulky shape at the bottom of the basement stairs of the house where I lived with my own children, it would always remind me of a coffin and of Martin, long dead by that time. I kept the pale blue wedding gown my mother made in it and remember to this day the smell of mothballs when I lifted the lid. Where is it now? Amy cleared out my apartment when I was first in the hospital, but that chest had been long gone before I went there.

1927. Ottawa. My mother at one end of the dinner table, my father at the other. I remember him on the street, his determined stride, the way he swung his walking stick, how proud he was and how inside him, like a tightly wound coil, was the deep and satisfied sense he held of himself. He was born in a time when roads were unpaved, when horse travel was common, and when streets were lit by kerosene, if at all. At the dinner table he and I were the quiet ones, the only family members who ate with an even pace, in the midst of the chattering crowd. Was it for this reason I was so unforgiving? My mother always considered him first and that expectation was passed on to his daughters. After I left home, I came to miss the velvet touch of her soft fingers on my skin as she'd fix my hem or straighten my collar and how she'd look at me closely and call me her 'girly' before I went out. But my father I remember preening before the mirror in the front hall, as I watched from the top of the stairs, my hand tightening on the rail.

After my mother died and he remarried and moved to Florida, I was the only family member who refused to meet his new wife, to visit him and marvel at his routine of walking on the beach before breakfast, even at ninety. I did this for my mother, for the memories I had of her sitting at the end of the table during our dinners, listening with her head tilted, offering calm reassurance and sympathy. She had become a large woman and wore long dresses with lace down the front and on the sleeves and collar. It was her way of caring for each of us, humming while she baked in the kitchen, that I always wanted to give to my own children. But it was my father who I was most like, who I understood with an instinct that, in later years, marked me as irascible, and allowed me to recognize treachery, perhaps even appreciate it.

The last evening I slept in my childhood house, the night before I married, alone in my small bedroom, I thought how now I would only be a visitor to those rooms. I did not know then, as I started out, that those rooms would be waiting for me to visit now, all these years later. But what good are these memories in the dark of my old age? Enough. I will turn on the television; the blur of faces, their gibberish, and my own inability to follow will fill these remaining moments before sleep overtakes me with its welcome amnesia.

Every death is a struggle lost. I heard these words, spoken by my sister Dorothy and as I lay alone pondering what they meant I saw her sitting in the reclining chair across the room. Somewhere in my mind I knew she'd been dead more than five years, and yet I also knew she was sitting quietly across from me. I accept such visitations these days, look forward to them even. We watched the television for a while and when the attendant came I thought she'd tell Dorothy to leave but she didn't notice her.

It was the Dorothy I knew when we were young, eighteen perhaps, dressed in a shift that our mother had made, her blonde hair pulled into a ponytail. She was so thin the armholes of her dress looped down five inches below her armpit and her long legs were bare. Once the TV was off and we were alone she spoke of her memories from our childhood. "You were Dad's favourite," she said in conclusion.

"You're crazy. We could barely stand each other."

"No, he used to watch you, praise you more than us. It was obvious."

She started to hum and I fell asleep to the sound. In the morning she was gone and the world was once again stark with sunlight when the morning attendant, a slight girl, no more than twenty, pushed the curtains open and said, "Good morning, June."

She helped me to the washroom. I'm slow now, I inch along, but I notice everything. In the washroom she bathed me, cleaned my soft skin, in places loose as dough, doused it with powder, and then brought me to the dining room for breakfast. I endure all this silently and feel like an old object, as most surely I am to these people hired to care for me. She walked back with me to my room where she propped me before the television. Another day to stack against all that have come before. I know there will not be many more to add. At times this thought leaves me weary and I push it aside but at other times, it is almost welcome.

At the table where I take my meals there are three other women. We eat in a room of twenty or so tables the same as ours. Mostly it is silent as we eat, and the sound of our eating seems to mask the nearly hundred lives crowded into that room like birds weaving nests from our pasts, artists with our medium the years of our lives, the places we've lived, the families we've lived with, all those holidays and lost routines.

Yesterday Sue came into the dining room, clapping her hands, "now, now, everyone, it's Edgar's birthday today; he's ninety-seven." Edgar was in a wheelchair, his head leaned to the left and back; he was drooling slightly. "Let's sing, everyone, Happy Birthday. Come on: Hap-p-p-y Birth-d-a-y to you." There was a mild response but most of us kept our heads down.

A few minutes later Amy came into the room, breathing heavily from the cold. Each time she arrives it takes a bit longer to focus on her face and comprehend what she is saying, and I worry someday I will not recognize her. And yet it may be a relief, giving up this pretense of understanding, of living in the present. When she approached me in the dining room, I saw something in her walk that reminded me of the child she had been, in the back yard, practising her majorette routine, twisting the baton and swinging it above her head. It had shiny stars embedded in the wand and rubber bulbs at each end with plastic tassels. The pompoms on her boots swung when she marched. She was earnest in her practice, ignoring the untidy yard as she jumped and slid and threw her arm over her head with the rotating baton. Watching her, everything else faded: the old chain link fences bent and broken, the weeds that overran the back path, the duplex facing our yard with its soiled veranda and awnings and the rusted cars in laneways. Against all that, she gleamed.

Her mitts were sticking out of her purse, the toque pushed back. She opened her jacket and smiled. "Hi Mom," she said and leaned down to kiss me.

Her cheek was cold. "Another miserable day, I take it," I said as she dragged a chair from the wall to sit beside me.

"Yeah, bad. Work was crazy too; sorry I couldn't get away sooner."

"Work," I said, "where do you work now?" As soon as I'd asked her I remembered I'd asked her this before, possibly every time she's mentioned work in the past year.

"Agriculture, Mom," it was the *Mom* that told me she'd noticed. Oh well, if that bothered her what would she think of Dorothy's visits, or the other people from my past who casually drop by. "So, Mom, how are you feeling?" she asked.

How am I feeling? In truth there is a change in my very bones, something wrong, an intrusion that will not leave, a haunting of sorts. I would explain it if I could, but it's as if a numbing poison has filtered into my blood that at times leaves me etherized. I could have said this to her and seen her face grow blank and uncertain. I could have, but there's no point; there's nothing to be done. I know this too. Besides she doesn't really want to know what is wrong, what can't be fixed. She wants me back in an apron in that 1959 kitchen where she ate her breakfasts before school, or years later when she was upstairs and I was downstairs talking on the phone to one of my sisters, just as I would have liked my mother back at the head of that dinner table. "Fine," I answered her.

⋇

Winter has always seemed for me like a country more than a season, a state of being more than a landscape. I've seen ninety of them, but this winter seems especially cruel. It is not only the ghosts from my past who appear to me, but the young versions of my own children visit at night; my daughter as a girl, dressed in a school jumper, the boys jostling and loud, "scuffamuttons" I called them. I will surface from moments in the kitchen of the house where they grew up and I will be here with another, older version of my daughter, frowning at me. She looks foreign, this woman, and yet there is still enough of the young girl to surprise me. "Hi, Mom," the conversation usually starts. But it's the young girl I miss, the smallness of her, braiding her hair in the morning sun, putting her to sleep in the evening. In the middle of the night when I awake and look up at the ceiling, when I can hear the traffic reduced to the rare careening stroke of sound, I can often hear her and her brother whispering and laughing in the corner of the room and I wonder how I will ever be able to say goodbye.

)X(

The next day I awoke into a fog. Amy's face came into view as she bent toward me; she had the pinched look of someone in pain, her eyes dark, an inversion of stars—she watched me with open sadness, not sure if I could see her. A few moments later she asked me how I was, but I didn't answer. She sat in the chair at the side of the bed and I forgot she was there, until one of the attendants came in and saw her, "Oh, Amy," she said. And I heard Amy respond, "It's like I'm losing her in stages; like she is being persuaded away from me and how I feel just isn't enough to keep her here."

"I know, I know," said this woman who did not in any true sense know, who saw in our situation what she sees all the time: a dying parent and a grieving child. Common and therefore simple. And it strikes me that what I've learnt is it's the love, the affection created over the years that is hard, permanent, far more permanent than those chairs, the bed, dresser that cluttered my hot room.

Still during the afternoon or the evening, when I close my eyes, a huge weariness overtakes me and I find myself back in my childhood home, in the upstairs hallway where I can hear my sisters in the kitchen, my father running water in the washroom, where the dust of a day in 1927 falls into the bands of light that stretch from the front room to fall before me. I hear my mother call and the sound seems to travel from a distance; there is warmth in the voice and perhaps the linger of a laugh, I hear it clearly as I answer her and descend the stairs.

EVANDIE

Evandie stood outside the glass shelter at the bus stop in a crowd of early morning commuters. It was a cold winter day and she'd heard on the radio before she left home that a snowstorm was expected to start before noon. A neighbour from the townhouse complex where she lived, a woman named Marianne, stood beside her. "Damn bus," she said. "What's taking it so long?" Evandie nodded and looked down the street toward the bend in the road as if her concentration alone could will the bus to appear. Both women were in their early forties, both formidable shapes in their bulky overcoats. Evandie wore a kerchief on her head, tucked into the collar. Under her coat she wore scrubs, the loose polyester trousers and smocks that all the attendants at the nursing home wore.

More than twenty years earlier, Evandie had moved to Ottawa from Montego Bay on the northeast coast of Jamaica. In Canada, during summer nights with the back door open for a breeze and the sound of the streets wafting in with the heat, Evandie would remember her first home—the surf, cars along the nearby boulevard, the sound of her younger brothers and sisters playing. Her husband grew up on the same block and it was he who convinced her to move to Ottawa, where he found a job providing maintenance for buses in a large depot. His name was Percival, and that was what Evandie called him, although his friends in Canada called him Percy. Like Evandie, he enjoyed living in Ottawa; he liked the camaraderie of his job and the neighbourhood where they lived, the rows of townhomes and the children in noisy groups playing on the sidewalks and parks. He and his friends, most of them immigrants who also found employment in the factories and warehouses of the same industrial park, would go out for a beer after work, or a baseball or hockey game on the weekend.

Evandie was a strong woman, five feet ten in her stocking feet, with a thick head of black hair and wide-set, chocolate brown eyes. The whites of her eyes were a creamy colour and her teeth flashed white when she smiled, which was often. By this winter day in 2006 Evandie had worked at Aldridge Lodge for six years. It was hard work: dressing patients, lifting them into wheelchairs, bringing them to the cafeteria or to the toilet and changing their diapers. Although there were parts of the job she found arduous, in general, she enjoyed the work for she knew how essential it was and how grateful some of the patients were, the women in particular. Those women who had spent their entire lives feeling in control of their own homes and who had held themselves straight and proud, now waited for the soft pad of Evandie's step and the comfort of her clear voice as she told them about the weather, the day's menu, or her own children.

Born and raised in a hot climate, Evandie didn't like the cold. But then not many people would have liked standing on that street corner, where the wind whipped across the adjacent field and swirled about the crowd as if they were pebbles in a frigid stream. People were rocking from foot to foot in an effort to stay warm, crossing their arms in front of them, stuffing their hands into their pockets, or sinking their chins into scarves around their necks.

She looked up at the sky, heavy with clouds. Snow was imminent. She thought about her favourite patient at the nursing home, June, a ninety-one-year-old woman who had moved in a year or so earlier. She'd noticed that lately June was spending her days drifting in and out of sleep, speaking less and less.

The ward where June lived and Evandie worked had twenty rooms off a long hallway, with a nurses' station in the center of the hall. Each room had a bathroom and a large window that looked out either to the grounds rimmed by a line of trees or a garden courtyard.

"I can't understand what's taking so long," Marianne said, as she put the hood of her jacket over her head. After a few minutes the bus turned the corner, and the young man standing close to them threw his cigarette on the ground, crushing it under his boot. On the bus, Evandie found a seat near the front by a window and, once settled, her thoughts turned again to June. During the months since she'd moved into the nursing home, Evandie and she had become friends of sorts. It made her happy to see June each morning, and she'd often think if something amused her during the day that she'd have to remember whatever it was to tell June. She spent hours listening to June's stories about when she was a young wife and mother or later when she was a widow—the life she had before the broken hip had made her bedridden.

Evandie too shared stories of her home and family, her life as a girl in Jamaica with her three sisters and four brothers. One morning while discussing their children, Evandie said, "My Mom still looks after kids, her grandkids mostly but also kids from the neighbourhood." Beside June's bed was a cart with a breakfast tray of boiled eggs, toast, and tea. She was sitting up in bed, smiling at Evandie. Always a petite woman, she now was tiny; *bird tiny*, Evandie thought, with twigs for fingers and the smallest of branches for arms.

"Seems there should be a time when that stops, but I guess for a mother, it never does," June said. That day her eyes were bright against her translucent skin and her face looked smooth and remarkably young, so that Evandie could see the girl she once was. "Children, they change everything." She picked up the spoon and scooped egg from the eggshell. "So tell me Evandie, what it was like growing up in Jamaica. Tell me about your mother." And Evandie sat at the end of her bed and recounted how she and her sisters used to play on the street until the night came in, how her mother's laugh and the sound of music filled their house. That had been a good day for June, a day when she was able to recount the stories of her life in a spirited way, full of humour, that hid, if only during the telling of them, the frailness of her body or her mind's increasing inability to concentrate.

※

One afternoon when Evandie was folding clothes on hangers and placing them in the wardrobe, June said, "I had a blender in my apartment in Montreal." Evandie was accustomed to conversations starting like this, without any obvious context. "I kept it on the counter beside the window that looked down into the back alleyway, by the fire escape."

"My Mom had an old blender too. She was given it by a woman she worked for," Evandie said as she folded trousers.

"One day when I moved something on the counter, a horrible black spider came out from behind it. I was alone, William was at work, the kids—I think Natalie was two by then and the baby must have been eight or nine months old—both of them were sleeping. And I screamed. God I remember how black it was against the white counter. Isn't that strange, to remember a spider after so many years?" Evandie thought, *it's going to be a good day, she wants to talk.*

"I always hated spiders; they scared me. When I was a kid I had to have one of my brothers get rid of them, but here I was alone in my apartment with my kids and I had to deal with it. So I took a serviette and you know the way they cringe down when you touch them, well I was able to grab it and put it outside. I was so proud of myself for dealing with that spider." She folded her fingers over the cuff of the blanket and looked toward the window. "Years later, of course, I had to deal with them by myself all the time, but this was my first time alone, and I remember it was that night that Will did not come home for dinner. He stopped for a drink at the pub and stayed, even after his buddies had left." Evandie raised the top of June's bed and June moved her arms to the outside of the blanket. "That day, the day I saw the spider, I made meatloaf, his favourite, and that's when it started, his coming home late. And when he did arrive home chances were he'd be drunk." June again turned toward the window, to where trees were shedding leaves and swaying in a strong autumn wind.

"Ah, yes," Evandie said with a sigh. "My Dad, well he used to come home often in that state—we just learned to stay clear." She stopped folding the clothes and remembered the night before, when her own husband had been drunk and fell asleep in the living room with the television blaring.

"That apartment in Montreal, I remember it well, the back stairs, I'd hear him come home and I'd pray he wasn't drunk." In the ensuing silence, sounds of the nursing home: the intercom, people in the hallway, televisions from nearby rooms, grew pronounced.

"So, what did you do?" Evandie said, resuming her folding. "I mean about his drinking?"

"Well, I tried to ignore it at first. Don't get me wrong, he was a good man. Good with the children and there were many happy times, it was to change, of course, when he became sick. But those days, when Natalie was a baby..."

June's voice trailed off and Evandie said, "Here, let me change the pillows." She rearranged June's position to make her more comfortable. "So when did you move back to Ottawa?" She went back to the wardrobe.

"When he became sick. TB. It was terrible back then, so many people died. We had to stay at his Mom's place and live in the basement with rooms separated by curtains." June leaned her head back and stared at the ceiling. "That was during the war. And after, when I got TB, his mother said Lawrence could stay, but not Natalie. Can you imagine, her own granddaughter?"

"That must have been hard, leaving them."

"Awful, just awful. They were so young." June's small feet under a blanket were peaked in front of her. "There's a time when you see what has to happen, when you realize you may not always be happy, that happiness somehow is no longer the point. Well, that's what happened to me in Montreal. Some people, like my sisters, would say I grew up."

Evandie stopped her folding, she knew what June meant; it had been a long time since she had thought of her own happiness. "So what was it like at the sanatorium?"

"We were forced to rest and there was supposed to be no excitement, but of course there was. It was a hotbed of gossip and intrigue." The tone of June's voice was now relaxed. "And that's where I met my second husband." Looking away, she smiled. "People didn't have as much as they do now. It was at the end of the war and it seemed everyone had a terrible story to tell." Yawning, she fell back into the bed. "You are such a sweet soul," she said, "listening to me like this."

Evandie closed the wardrobe doors and walked back to the bed where June had closed her eyes and fallen asleep. Over the years, she'd come to recognize the way death comes in, the patient's slow retreat inward, coupled with an unwillingness to speak and on other days a sleepiness so profound it was impossible to wake. At times, like this day for June, there would be a reprieve and almost a joy in the recounting of their lives, days when they'd accept a cup of tea or cookie and sit up, alert, and want the lights on. But always other days followed, when it was impossible to rouse them and Evandie saw in sleep's irresistible persuasion the final lull that would steal them from their life and families.

The bus was waiting at a stoplight when it began to snow. The driver turned on the wipers that swept across the two large windows in front of him. Evandie moved her purse closer to her chest and thought, *this is going to make me even later.* She could see children on the sidewalk, walking backward against the wind and snow. They reminded her of her daughter Carolyna and then of the night before.

Percy and a friend had been sitting in the two easy chairs facing the television in their living room when Evandie returned from work. They were dressed in their work clothes, flannel shirts, overalls and heavy socks, drinking beer and laughing as they tried to blow up balloons for Carolyna. "Here, here, you go," Percy's friend said as he tied the stem of a red balloon and passed it to her, and then, "Well looky here, if it isn't the missus," when he saw Evandie stomping snow off her boots in the hallway.

She had walked from the bus, carrying grocery bags of food for dinner, and when she opened the door to a mess of coats and scarves, she smelled beer. She let go of the bags and put her mittened hands to her cold ears. "Percival," she said, "can I speak to you?"

"Sure, doll," he said, yanking the chair's lever down so that he could follow her.

In the kitchen, she said, "I need a bit of help here."

"Alrighty, hon, once Jack leaves, I'm all yours."

"And when will that be?"

"Soon, once the show's over."

His eyes were rimmed in red, he was grinning and Evandie was reminded of the young man he had been in Jamaica, when he was full of plans. He'd knock on her back door, jumpy and animated, and her father would say dismissively, "Evandie, it's your young man." Even then, years before they were married, she found it difficult to stay angry with him.

"Okay, Evey. Just start dinner and we can talk later." And Evandie let him go back to the living room, was in fact glad to see him leave so she could be alone in the kitchen she loved with its new appliances, its island counter and large window that looked out onto the neighbourhood park.

⋇

On the bus, Evandie watched the snow accumulate in lines at the wipers' edge. Marianne, who was sitting behind her, moved forward in the seat and because they were stopped for no perceptible reason, said, "Must be an accident up there." The snow was growing heavy so that they were unable to see beyond a few cars ahead of them. Evandie leaned back and remembered the day before, when June's daughters had mentioned their mother's condition, that she was sleeping most of the day and not wanting to eat. Evandie told them it was normal. "She's had a long life," she said. "You have to expect some days all she'll want is sleep."

The bus route did not travel into the grounds of the nursing home so Evandie was forced to trudge along the long pathway from the bus stop to the central entrance. The snow had drifted into peaked mounds and the winter trees stood strong above her, their branches interlaced. When she reached the front door she stopped and took off her scarf, which was encrusted with snow, shaking it out in the vestibule.

"Look at it out there," one of the doctors said on the way to his car, but there was a gay tone in his voice. When Evandie had first moved here, she was surprised by how storms of this sort often filled people with a sort of excitement or enthusiasm. She hurried to the nurses' station, dragging her scarf behind her, calling out "hello" and "good morning" to patients and co-workers.

The attendant she was replacing was writing at the desk, her head down, and when she heard Evandie, she said, "Hi there. Has it started to snow yet?"

"Yes, crazy out there. I'm so sorry to be late; there was some kind of accident." Evandie said. She hung up her coat and bent to remove her boots when she heard the woman, without raising her head, say, "June Grosford died twenty minutes ago."

"What?"

"Yeah, the family was called in the night and the doctor just left."

Evandie stood with one hand on the wall to balance herself, the other still holding a boot.

※

After June's family left, Evandie visited the room where June's body was resting, the covers pulled to her chin, her knees still raised on a pillow as they were in life to give her comfort. Evandie had often placed her in just this position, so that once she was without pain, she could fall asleep. And that was how she looked, pain-free and sleeping. There was a smell of antiseptic in the room, subtle but distinct. The sounds of the hall, an intercom, the call for an attendant, the scuttle of wheelchairs and the pill dispenser cart, all disappeared, and Evandie herself with her soft-soled shoes did not make a sound as she approached the bed. She leaned down close to June, as she had done so often in the past, when she attempted to wake or entice her to eat or drink. June's skin was smooth, erased of strain or expression and there was no flutter to her eyelids, only stillness, an extension of the room and white light from the window that looked out onto the snowy courtyard.

June's body held something of the miraculous. Looking at her this closely, Evandie was left with a sense of all she could not know. The woman June had been, those years that stretched back to the early 1900s, lay calm and lost, and in the calm was the notion that June's death was as it was meant to be. In this stillness, before June's past and memories would be subsumed by the crush of time, something of their essence still hung in the room, like the sound of her voice.

In the early evening of that February day, Evandie sat on the bus on her way home, tired, her feet hurting and with a pain in her shoulder that made it difficult to turn quickly. *Five o'clock*, she thought, *and already dark*. Snow fell softly. Between stops, the bus driver turned off the aisle lights and for a few minutes Evandie watched the houses, strip malls and apartment buildings pass by. She held her purse on her lap. When she closed her eyes and heard the rattle of the bus and muted conversations of the other passengers, she thought of the slant of winter light and the silence that had filled June's room. Then she thought of Carolyna, who she knew at that moment was listening to Percival and his friend in the living room, a night like so many before it, and so many to follow, a night so ordinary that in the future it would be completely forgotten. Evandie tucked her chin into the collar of her coat as the bus, with each stop and lurch forward, moved her closer and closer to home.

WEEKEND

On a sunny Saturday morning in July, Thomas and Vanessa, both in their late twenties, sat side by side in Thomas's Toyota, the car he'd bought when he was at university six years earlier that was old even then. They were on their way to visit his mother, and although Vanessa had spoken with her on the phone many times during the year she'd been living with Thomas, they'd never met. The car rattled, and Vanessa tried to find the source by placing her palm on sections of the dashboard. "I hate that sound," she said.

The sky above, seared by the circle of sun, filtered to the palest blue at the horizon. Laid out before them, the road between Kingston and Ottawa stretched in long, straight miles of gray pavement. "Monotonous," Vanessa said.

Thomas turned to her and smiled. "Who, me?"

"No, silly."

When Thomas had called a week earlier to tell his mother, Amy, that they planned to marry, she congratulated him and said they should visit the following weekend. "I know, I know, you've been busy with the new place and all, but it's been almost a month and you haven't made it here yet." Dressing for the trip,

Vanessa changed three times before settling on white capri pants and a pale blue T-shirt. She was tall, her body flat with the straight lines of a teenager, and her blonde hair was pulled into a ponytail. She wore flip-flops accented by a cluster of rhinestones, and she kept taking the shoes off and putting them back on, tucking her long legs under her, and then stretching them out in front of her.

"Don't worry," Thomas said. "She's going to adore you." He knew that even if his mother didn't approve of Vanessa, his feelings would not change; he'd chosen her and would give up anyone to be with her. These thoughts made him feel expansive and confident, so that he hummed and drove quickly with a lightness of spirit, finding in the flow of traffic, in the music on the radio, and in the way Vanessa fidgeted beside him, evidence of an overriding happiness.

Vanessa's mother had died at fifty-three, when Vanessa was in high school, and for the last year her father had been living in a retirement home in Scarborough, outside Toronto. A month earlier, when Vanessa and Thomas were driving from Edmonton where they'd met, to their new jobs and home in Kingston, they stopped to visit her father. Vanessa's sister Pat met them at the retirement home, and at the hottest hour of the day the four of them sat in the garden, a fenced area behind the building. There they spoke for over an hour, while Thomas told them about his mother, who worked for the government in Ottawa, and his father, who lived outside the city with his second wife, in the same small village where Thomas had grown up. What he did not say was that he still avoided thinking about his father with his new wife, and that when he did it seemed that the anger he'd known when his parents first separated had been replaced by a complicated regret, feelings he found easier not to contemplate.

Later, as they continued their drive to Kingston, Vanessa told Thomas that Pat had called him a charmer. "But what does she know?" She smiled over at him, touching the side of his face, but he didn't answer and kept his gaze on the two lanes of traffic before him. He turned on the radio, and although he looked to Vanessa as if he had nothing on his mind but driving, he was thinking about Vanessa's father, realizing he had no clear idea what the frail, tired man had thought of him. In the courtyard they'd sat beneath an umbrella, while her father smoked, something his daughters chided him about. The sun lit the brilliant red of geraniums in flowerpots and the emerald of the grass where patches of sunlight pooled. It was June, one of the first hot days of the year, and when Pat made a comment about the summer being a long time coming, Thomas agreed. Glancing at Vanessa's father, he saw a flicker of derision on his face, a dismissal of their bland conversation, and by extension, of Thomas himself. He grew quiet, sensing that Vanessa's father had recognized something of Thomas's own fear that his civility and conventionality were a thin veneer that barely hid the fact that he could appear ludicrous at times, deferential in his interactions, especially with women. The thought spread through him like a fire let loose, making his glance shift from the garden to the nearby thoroughfare where cars raced by, until Pat called him back with a question about how he'd met Vanessa.

The thought of Vanessa, how the world paled when compared to her, filled him with enthusiasm to tell the story of their first meeting in the office of the engineering firm where he worked after graduating, so that he felt restored to his former sanguinity and the day became bright again. The story made Pat and Vanessa laugh. Even Vanessa's father was smiling, and Thomas wondered if perhaps he had misread him. It was only later that Thomas felt again the father's disapproval and a concern that in the years to come, despite Vanessa's coaxing, he would never feel close to him. Now, a month later, when they'd settled into their new jobs in Kingston and moved into an old house they were spending their weekends renovating, they were again on a highway, travelling to meet another parent, an occasion that would further solidify them as a couple and make it clear their allegiances were now primarily to each other.

Thomas was surprised when his mother opened the door to them. Her hair was past her shoulders, longer than he'd ever seen it, and was a pale honey colour. She was wearing makeup, which surprised him also, and she looked fit in her jeans and T-shirt, slimmer than the last time he'd seen her, which had been at the funeral of his grandmother, more than a year earlier.

"Oh, my, let me get a look at the two of you," she said, drawing Thomas to her and giving him a hug. "And Vanessa, how nice to finally meet face-to-face." She turned to Vanessa and held her at arm's length for a moment before hugging her. When Thomas glanced into the apartment, he saw Paul, his mother's boyfriend, seated at the kitchen table, a glass of wine and a partially eaten sandwich on a plate before him. Paul stood and walked toward the hallway, smiling. Of average height, he had light brown hair and was dressed in jeans and a pale blue shirt. Thomas thought he looked like a model for casual attire, and yet something too precise in the crease of his shirt, in the fade of his jeans, gave an impression that was the opposite of casual.

"Tom, I think you met Paul at the funeral last year," Amy said.

"Yes, yes, we met briefly," Tom said, leaning in to shake Paul's hand.

Thomas knew his mother had been seeing Paul for a while and it was because she spent last Christmas with him that Thomas had made an excuse to avoid returning home.

Paul clutched Tom's hand tightly and both men stared long enough at each other for an uncomfortable silence to settle, broken finally when Amy said, "But Paul I think you haven't met Vanessa". Vanessa smiled and Amy noticed her white even teeth. "So where's your bag?" she said.

"In the car. I'll get it in a minute," Thomas said.

"We've planned a dinner out tonight," Amy said as they moved into the kitchen from the hall, "at a restaurant in the market."

Paul said, "My daughter, Karen—she's your age, Tom—she's going to meet us there."

"Oh, really, how nice." But a prickly sensation at the back of his neck made Tom's look darken. Amy put her arm around his shoulder and said, "My boy. Isn't he wonderful?"

)(

There can be nothing more intriguing, Amy thought, than those moments when you notice your child has changed, that his features have broadened, his beard thickened, his hair turned a darker shade, that through these and other less obvious changes, like a turn of phrase or a new thoughtful expression, he has moved away from you, moved away from being at your side to being before you, a person with opinions and thoughts of his own. She was thinking how happy, how truly happy, she was that he was with her and in that instant felt a sensation bordering on awe, so that she put her arm around his shoulder and said again, "My boy."

A moment later she was putting together plates of cold chicken and roast beef, bowls of coleslaw, macaroni and potato salads, the salads her mother had always made and that were Thomas's favorites. He had gone to fetch their suitcase from the car, and Vanessa was helping to carry the plates from the fridge to the table. Paul stood by the door, talking to Vanessa. "Sorry I didn't wait for you two."

"Well, we didn't even know when we'd be here; it's kind of hard to tell, with the traffic and all." With the counters crowded with utensils and food and the flowered curtains flowing over the sink into the room, Vanessa found the kitchen cramped. She too had been surprised by Amy. She expected someone more serious, statelier in appearance, not this woman who moved quickly from the fridge to table, who pushed Paul with a playful shove and said, "Okay, mister, you're in the way. Make yourself scarce."

When they were alone in the kitchen, Amy asked Vanessa, "So, have you chosen a date yet?" She stopped setting the table, looked at the young woman who at that moment was pulling a strand of hair behind her ear, and Amy thought how she would not have chosen this thin, tall girl for her son.

Thomas came into the kitchen and said, "I told you, it'll be next September, but we haven't chosen the day." Amy recognized the harsh tone of willfulness that in his youth had always meant he was angry.

"Come with me, Thomas," she said, "I'll show you where you two will be sleeping." Thomas knew the spare room, it was where he slept when he visited, but he followed his mother. "Are you okay?" she said when they were alone.

"Yeah, of course, what do you mean?"

"You seem upset."

"Why would I be upset?" He put his bag on the bed. "I'm a little disappointed, that's all, that my mother and my future wife won't be spending time alone."

"Oh, I see. It's Paul."

"It's not about him, specifically. I'm sure he's great, but for this weekend, don't you think . . ."

"Don't I think what, Thomas? Seeing as I'm meeting your girlfriend, I thought you'd like to spend some time with my boyfriend." They both stood looking down at the bag on the bed. "This is the longest we've ever gone without seeing each other, Tom, and I don't like it." She turned to look at him. "I don't like that you don't know Paul, that you don't know what he means to me."

"Forget it, Mom, just forget it."

Amy left the room and went to the washroom, standing with her back to the door. Her heart was pounding and her eyes stung from the threat of tears.

⁕

The restaurant was crowded and dark, lit by candles and dim overhead lamps. When Karen was late Paul called her cell phone but there was no answer. "She must be lost; she doesn't know this part of the city well." They were seated in the middle of a crowded room with a chair left empty at the end of the table.

Earlier in the day, Amy, Thomas, and Vanessa had visited the grave of Amy's mother, June, in Beechwood Cemetery. The sun fell in puddles of light, touching the tombs scattered like stones on a wide shore. Amy had always liked the randomness of this cemetery; it seemed fitting to her that the stones meandered over the fields in a haphazard way. June was buried with Amy's aunt Margaret, who had bought a plot for four more than seventy years before when she was married to her first husband.

By the graveside, the sun poured on their skin as if it were hot honey, in the eerie quieting of the place, it seemed to Thomas as if the wind was made of a thousand voices. And yet he knew it was really only the sound of it caught in the high branches, jittering the leaves and jostling the bushes along the road. They looked down in silence to the head and foot stones and Thomas thought of his grandmother as he had known her. He thought of Christmas dinners spent at Amy's cousin Sophia's house, when his grandmother and her sisters would gather together, laughing and recalling the stories from their youth, the way the city had looked in the 1920s and 30s, the marriages and children since. *But she was real,* Thomas thought, kneeling to push leaves from the foot stone with her name, just as real as Aunt Margaret with her long cigarette holder, an object that fascinated him when he was a young boy. And just as real, he thought, as all those names on all those stones that surrounded him where he knelt; all signified lives lived, stretching back into past decades and centuries. They all ate dinners at night, breakfasts in the morning, worked at something dear to them, experienced special times when a child was born, or a parent died, all held these moments of love earned or denied. The clattering cacophony of their lives caught in the hot stillness of this simple Saturday afternoon.

"I didn't know grandma was buried with Aunt Margaret."

"That's right, you had to rush off," Amy said.

"I had a plane to catch, Mom, remember?"

"This is a pretty place," Vanessa said. She missed Paul, who had gone back to his apartment to get ready for dinner. She missed the way he put her at ease, with his effortless conversation that filled in the awkward moments. Thomas with his mother made Vanessa nervous; there seemed to be a new harshness to him, something pointed and tinged with anger which excluded her. "Bit full of himself, isn't he?" he said about Paul when they were alone getting ready to go out. If it weren't for her attempts to keep the conversation light, she knew Thomas and his mother would be letting whatever lingered between them sink the day into unhappiness.

"Oh, yes, it's nice," Amy said, but she thought, *Can't she say anything more insightful?*

Karen arrived half an hour late; Paul was right, she'd been lost. Thomas wasn't sure if it was the fuchsia shirt she was wearing and flowered culottes, but the room suddenly seemed full of her and her exuberance. Her arms were puffy like the arms of a doll with twist-on hands; Thomas noticed because she kept her elbows on the table and spoke with her palms open. He thought she'd already been drinking and then with them she drank two glasses of red wine in quick succession.

"So, Vanessa, what do you think of Ottawa?" she asked, and before Vanessa could answer she moved to Thomas. "And Thomas, Dad said you're a city planner." Karen didn't seem to notice Thomas's reluctance to say more after a noncommittal "yes," as she continued the conversation with a lengthy description of her own job as a legal assistant, ending with, "And Vanessa, you're a physiotherapist, right?"

Paul's glance never left his daughter's face, nor did his smile diminish, and he'd mouth certain words she was about to say. Amy had often witnessed the attention Paul paid his youngest daughter, and she knew he did this because Karen was the only one of his three children who had not refused to see him after he separated from their mother. She could see Thomas judging Karen, as she herself had initially judged her, as willful and self-absorbed.

When they were almost finished dinner and Karen had started on her third glass of wine, she said, "So, what do you think, Thomas, about my dad and your mom? Kind of weird, eh?"

Amy's fork hit her plate and she looked toward Karen who kept her attention on Thomas.

"Weird, how?" Thomas said.

"Well, weird, to think at their age, you know," she turned now from Thomas to look at Amy, her eyelids drooping. "I mean it's kind of creepy to think about." She was holding her glass of wine precariously with two fingers while leaning across the table. "I mean, don't you think it's kind of perverse?"

"I don't know, no, I don't think so," Thomas said. The table had become quiet, and he thought that this must have been what she wanted to say since she arrived.

Alert to the new tone in the conversation, Paul said, "I don't think Karen meant anything by what she said, did you, Karen?"

"Of course not. Why is everyone so serious?" Karen said. "I just thought you'd agree, Tom, what with the two of us being from broken homes, that you'd see it the way I do." The sound of muted conversations, the low utterance of music and utensils on plates, crowded around them. "I guess it's because I was just at my mother's house before I came here and saw how she was going to have dinner alone, and look at us, living it up, out on the town."

"Karen, please."

"Please what, Dad?" She turned to look at him for the first time since sitting down. "Please don't have an opinion? Please be quiet?" Her face was scalded with indignation. But she quickly smiled and looked at her glass. "I'm probably too old for this tantrum."

"Look, Karen," Thomas said, leaning toward her, "if it makes you feel any better, I know what you're saying. It's difficult, but it gets easier." Thomas straightened and looked at his mother, "And besides everyone deserves happiness."

Karen lowered her gaze to her plate until Vanessa said, "We were thinking of taking a detour to where Thomas grew up if we have time tomorrow."

"You should visit your father," Amy said to Thomas who grimaced and said, "One parent at a time, Mom." But he felt warm toward his mother and even toward Karen and Paul, who were now avoiding eye contact, sitting back in their chairs like petulant children. In this moment Thomas could see the family resemblance, the curve of the skin over the eye and the colour of hair, and he felt that he knew them and in this knowledge a spontaneous sympathy bloomed.

They didn't order dessert; everyone said they were full. Karen decided to stay uptown at her father's apartment, and so Vanessa, Thomas, and Amy went back to Amy's apartment without them.

At two in the morning Amy awoke. Her bedroom window was open and she felt the breeze from the street and heard the sound of cars from the busy intersection nearby. The branches from the large oak trees before her window swayed, casting moving shadows into the room. She went to the kitchen and sat at the table, her slippered feet on a chair, a glass of orange juice in front of her. A little while later, she heard someone get up to use the washroom and then heard sounds in the hallway. "Hello," she said when she saw Vanessa. "Couldn't sleep?"

"I always have trouble in a new place."

"Plus, I'm sure you're wondering what kind of family you're marrying into." Amy looked down at the table, running her finger along the rim of her glass. Vanessa leaned against the doorway watching her. The moon was full and white light drifted idly through the open window.

When Vanessa came into the room, Amy moved her feet to make room at the table. "Please," Amy lifted the orange juice container toward her, "have some."

Vanessa poured a glass. "You know, I read that men are often attracted to women who are like their mothers," she said. "But I don't think that's the case here, do you?"

"Oh, I don't know," Amy said. "I think if you'd known me at your age, we wouldn't seem so different."

"Really?"

She doesn't believe me, Amy thought. *She doesn't think she could ever find herself at my age, living this kind of life.* And in recognizing Vanessa's youth Amy felt protective toward her and said, "Well, it's true. It's the things that happen that change you. And I guess there's not much sense questioning them." She leaned forward bracing her forearms on the table edge. "Because without that, I wouldn't be here right now, enjoying this night, enjoying you."

"Is that what you're doing?" Vanessa smiled, and Amy thought how pretty she was, she'd missed that somehow during the day, but here in the cool air of late night, with Vanessa in a short nightgown, her feet bare and face scrubbed, she looked younger, her skin flawless, her grey-blue eyes clear.

"Oh, yes, Vanessa, I'm enjoying myself these days, enjoying seeing my son become a man, and for the role you play in that, among other things, enjoying you."

They heard the sudden singing and hollering of a crowd that had gathered on the street and then someone yelling for them to be quiet. "What's that?" Vanessa said.

"The bars are just closing. Happens every weekend. I don't even hear it anymore."

"It sounds happy."

"Yes, doesn't it? I quite like the sound, especially when I'm here alone."

The noise from the street woke Thomas, who came into the kitchen rubbing his eyes. "What are you guys doing here?" he said. "Hatching some kind of plot?" He poured himself a glass of juice as both women watched him. Leaning on the counter, after a few moments with no one speaking and the sounds from the street filling the space between them, he said, "I'm going back to bed." He ran his hand through his hair, a gesture Amy had seen him make since he was a young boy. "And you two can both stay here and continue whatever scheming you were up to." His voice was relaxed and held the promise of a laugh.

The next morning Vanessa and Thomas left after breakfast. Rain had moved in, and dark clouds mottled the sky. Amy saw those clouds from her kitchen window hanging low over the view of patched backyards with paint-chipped fences and wooden porches. She walked Thomas and Vanessa to their car and kissed them both goodbye. "You must visit us," Vanessa said and took Amy's hand before settling in the passenger seat beside Thomas.

An hour later when Amy was alone, cleaning the dishes, Paul called. She saw the number on the phone display but didn't answer. When he called again, two hours later, she wasn't at home. She'd gone for a walk in the rain. Under an umbrella, seeing houses stacked along the street, cars parked in lane ways, wet trees swaying above, she thought about the town where she'd lived when Thomas was young, and where he and Vanessa were now visiting. *Thomas,* she thought, *still my boy,* and remembered how he had walked away from her and Vanessa when they were by her mother's grave, how he stood before other stones reading the names and dates. He did not say anything, but Amy knew he was contemplating the wide, chaotic life that existed for each person between the dates of their birth and death. It touched her now with something like regret that life comes with such contradictions, that happiness is tinged with the thought of its end and that she could not protect him from any of it.

Beneath the umbrella Amy felt safe from the rain which had begun to fall harder. She turned at the canal and walked beside the concrete posts and black railings, the rain making dents in the moving water. It was a warm rain though, and she felt warmed too from her thoughts of the previous day, and then in her imagining she saw Vanessa at that moment in her glittering shoes listening to Thomas. They would be in the car, side by side, and Amy knew that when they laughed and recounted the evening spent with Karen and Paul—how maudlin Karen had become, how serious Paul was—that Vanessa would be so happy to have the old Thomas back.

ACKNOWLEDGEMENTS

For careful and compassionate reading of my stories, I would like to thank: Frances Boyle, Jean Van Loon, Sonia Tilson, Ann Cavlovic, Liz McKeen, Kathryn Mulvihill, Mary Lee Bragg, Lesley Buxton, Jenny Green, Colleen Pellatt, Kelly Patterson, Sandra MacPherson, Patricia Lindsey, Wendy Brandts, and Mary Borsky (workshop leader). And for their writing insights and wisdom, I also thank The Rubies: Lise Rochefort, Laurie Koensgen, Claudia Radmore, Robin MacDonald, Jacqueline Bourque, and Pearl Pirie. I would also like to express my profound gratitude to David Staines (and Elizabeth Hay and John Lacharity for bringing us together) for his insightful comments and assistance. I am also indebted to Tom Jenks, Antanas Sileika, Bonnie Burnard and Guy Vanderhaeghe for their support and encouragement during the writing of these stories.

To the most generous of mentors, Isabel Huggan, I give my warmest thanks and deep affection. For his encouragement over the years I'd also like to thank Ian Colford and for the boundless support of my family and friends, I am indebted forever.

I'd also like to acknowledge Ingeborg Boyens and the fine souls at Great Plains Publications for their sensitive reading and support of this book.

And to my first reader and editor, André Savary, my deepest love and gratitude. I thank him for all that he has done to make this book possible and all the happiness and laughter he has brought to my life.

Earlier versions of stories in this collection first appeared in the following:

"Weekend," *Narrative Magazine* 2011
"Studebaker," *Fiddlehead* 2010
"Nelson Street," *Missouri Review* 2009
"The Murder on Prince Albert Street," *Windsor Review* 2009
"The View from the Lane," *Descant* 2005
"The Worst Snowstorm of the Year," *Other Voices* 2005
"My Brother's Condition," *Antigonish Review* 2003
I thank the editors of these magazines.

Excerpt from "On the Night of the First Snow, Thinking about Tennessee" from SESTETS: POEMS by Charles Wright. Copyright © 2009 by Charles Wright. Reprinted by permission of Farrar, Straus and Giroux, LLC.